HEATHER GREER

Scrivenings
PRESS
Quench your thirst for story.
www.ScriveningsPress.com

Published by Scrivenings Press LLC
15 Lucky Lane
Morrilton, Arkansas 72110
https://ScriveningsPress.com

Printed in the United States of America

Paperback ISBN 978-1-64917-137-5

eBook ISBN 978-1-64917-138-2

Library of Congress Control Number: 2021940991

Cover by Linda Fulkerson
www.bookmarketinggraphics.com

Scripture taken from the NEW AMERICAN STANDARD BIBLE(r), Copyright (c) 1960,1962,1963,1968,1971,1972,1973,1975,1977 by The Lockman Foundation. Used by permission. www.lockman.org.

To those of us who have struggled trusting that God's dreams for us are even better than our own.

"'For I know the plans that I have for you,' declares the LORD, 'plans for welfare and not for calamity to give you a future and a hope.'"
Jeremiah 29:11 (NASB)

ACKNOWLEDGMENTS

I thank God for the ability to do what I'm passionate about while sharing His message with others and for giving me the best support around in my family, the Carbondale Christian Writers Group, and the Once Upon a Page girls. You all rock!

Thank you to Linda and Shannon for giving this book a home at Scrivenings Press and for pushing me to make it the best it can be.

And special thanks to the readers. Without you, I wouldn't be allowed to do what I do. Thank you!

1

The stainless-steel mixing bowls crashed together like gongs hammered by rhythm-challenged children as Livvy shoved them into the lower cabinet and forced the door shut. She huffed out a hot breath. This wasn't her, not by a long shot. Livvy worked hard to afford quality equipment, and she took care of it. She had to for The Sugar Cube to compete successfully in the fast-paced St. Louis food truck scene. She'd planned everything to the last penny before investing her meager life savings as the down payment on her loan, and now it was all going sideways like that hubcap mishap last year.

Regretting her moment of temper, Livvy opened the cabinet and began rearranging the bowls until they fit perfectly.

"What's wrong? This is an awesome opportunity."

Tabitha sat perched on a stool in the corner, her full lips turned down as she tapped a long envelope against her leg.

Livvy rubbed her hands down the front of her polka-dotted apron and tightened the strings around her waist, then grabbed a bottle of cleaner and a rag. "It seems like a great opportunity, but what if I'm not good enough?"

"Oh, please." Tabitha massaged her temples and groaned. She shook the paper in Livvy's direction, volume rising with her intensity. "This. This right here says you're good enough. Your invitation to the big leagues. Do you know how many people didn't get this? A lot. You're one of ten, out of probably hundreds."

With her hand poised above the counter, Livvy stopped, her fingers on the trigger of the spray bottle. Tabitha didn't get worked up. In all the years they'd known each other, Livvy was the one who got in trouble for talking out of turn. Livvy was the one front and center in their friendship, while Tabitha was content to take everything in. When Livvy's parents died, Tabitha was the calm in her storm, and now her calm was thundering. Still. She had to think about her business.

"You know it's not as easy as closing up shop and entering the competition, even if they are taping the show during my slow months of December and January."

A raised brow. "And why not?"

"Loan payments come due the 15th. Every month. Whether The Sugar Cube is earning anything or not."

"I know that."

"Not once have I ever failed to make my loan payments." Livvy looked up at the ceiling and blinked back tears of frustration before refocusing on Tabitha. She shook her head and swallowed the lump in her throat. "I've not even been late. God has blessed this venture so much. But all that time out of commission when the transmission went out, and what it cost to fix! I didn't have a lot in savings, but now ..."

Livvy had to look away from Tabitha's sad puppy eyes before tears sprang up again. She squirted the already sparkling wood counter and began scrubbing it mercilessly. "Maybe I'm supposed to take the hint. If I take a chance right now and fail, with no safety net, The Sugar Cube is gone."

"You can do this." Tabitha stilled her hand. "*Cake That* is a once-in-a-lifetime opportunity, and risks go both ways. It would put the Sugar Cube on the national stage, and winning one hundred thousand dollars would pay off the twenty-five thousand you owe the bank. You could lease the storefront you've been drooling over."

Livvy didn't look up. Success in the competition would also be the perfect way to honor her mother's belief in her, to prove Livvy was doing what she was meant to do.

"What if I lose?"

Tabitha swatted the idea from the air with the back of her hand. "Olivia Rae Miller, not going to happen. Cupcakes have been your life almost as long as we've been friends. You're an amazing baker."

"Still ..."

"If you need someone else's opinion, fine." Tabitha cleared her throat as she raised the letter from her lap. "Your submission video was truly one of a kind. Members of our production crew spent time in St. Louis recently to sample your cupcakes and speak with your customers. Your reputation with your clientele is unmatched, and your skill as a baker is evident in each bite. It is our honor to invite you to join us for the second season of *Cake That.'*"

Nothing else needed to be said for Livvy to hear *I told you so* loud and clear. The show wanted her. In only a few weeks, she could be on a nationally televised baking competition.

Reluctant excitement bubbled up inside Livvy. Whether she participated or not, it was an honor to be chosen. Simply thinking about going to California and proving to herself that she belonged in the baking world she loved was thrilling.

"This is completely unreal! I've read it over and over, and I still can't believe it. It sounds like they really did like what they sampled."

"Why wouldn't they? We know you make the best cupcakes in St. Louis. This is your chance to prove they're the best in the whole United States. You have to do this."

"But I'll have to shut down for weeks while I'm away—"

"Are you going somewhere, Miss Livvy?"

Livvy shot Tabitha a reproving look and glanced at the clock on the wall. Whether they were finished with the discussion or not, it was time to open for business.

"How lucky am I?" Livvy smiled and turned her attention to the petite ballerina on the other side of her counter. "My first customer of the day is also my favorite. And I'll guess you did a great job at dance class today and earned yourself a treat. Am I right, Abbie?"

Tight black braids bounced up and down as the little girl nodded. "Yep. Mama said I could pick anything since I did so good at practice. I'm glad you were here today. You weren't in your spot last week after class. I've got a surprise for you. I'm going to be a swan princess in the recital next week. You should come see me. Mama says I dance better than any of the other swans. Did you ever dance, Miss Livvy? I love to dance."

Livvy fought back the giggle building in her throat, locking eyes with the girl's mother fighting the same battle. Abbie was completely serious and unaware of how adorable she was.

"No. I never learned to dance, at least not for real like you. I spent most of my time in the kitchen learning to bake cupcakes."

Suddenly Tabitha stood beside her. "And that is why Miss Livvy just got invited to be a contestant on *Cake That*."

Livvy glared at her. Why was Tabitha getting out of her self-imposed social bubble to talk to people? Oh yeah, to push an idea Livvy wasn't sold on.

"*Cake That?*"

"It's a television show where bakers compete to see who can bake the best cakes and cupcakes."

"You're going to be on television Miss Livvy?" Abbie's dark brown eyes grew large.

A less-than-innocent nod from Tabitha earned her a kick in the foot from Livvy behind the counter. Too bad all Abbie saw was the excitement in Tabitha's face.

"Wow! I've never been on television before. When I'm a

prima ballerina I will be. Everyone will want to interview me and watch me dance. You're so lucky, Miss Livvy. "

"I've been invited, but I haven't decided if I'm going to go. The show takes several weeks to record. That's a lot of time without The Sugar Cube being open for business. Do you think you can go that long without one of my cupcakes?"

"Sure, Miss Livvy. I'll just eat a whole bunch when you get back. Mama says when you've got it, you've got to share it. That's what she tells me about dancing, and you're good at cupcakes like I'm good at dancing. So, you've got to share it, too."

Abbie's mother placed a restraining hand on the little girl's shoulder, though her attention remained trained on Livvy. "As you can see, Abbie doesn't have a problem sharing much of anything. But she's right, you know. Chances like this don't come along very often. I really think you should consider going."

As much as she loved Abbie and her mother after months of having them as regular customers, Livvy couldn't get into her concerns with them.

"You're right. This is a once-in-a-lifetime opportunity, and I plan to consider all pros and cons of going before I make my final decision. Now, I think we owe a little prima ballerina a special treat, and I have the perfect cupcake in mind."

Livvy knew without asking which cupcake to pull from the display case. She'd learned Abbie's favorite flavors in the first month The Sugar Cube was open for business. Today's cupcake would also appeal to her love of all things girly.

"A pretty princess cupcake for the prettiest swan princess in the ballet." She extended the sweet confection across the counter. Topped with a silky swirl of pink strawberry buttercream frosting and dotted with light purple sugar pearls and a fine dusting of iridescent powder, the cupcake was fit for ballet royalty and decorated with Abbie in mind.

The child's lips formed an *o* as she reached out to take the cupcake with something akin to reverence. "Is it strawberry?"

"Of course. Would I give you anything else?"

"How much do I owe you today?" Her mother moved up to the counter.

"For my favorite little dancer? It's on the house." She looked at Abbie as her tongue swirled through the sweet frosting. "Just remember to mention me when you grow up to be a famous ballerina."

"I am going to be famous one day." She smacked her lips as she chased escaped frosting around with her tongue before smiling brightly. "Just you wait and see."

Livvy laughed. "I have no doubt about that. You're already a star in my book, Miss Abbie."

"What do you say, Abbie?" Her mother nudged the little girl's shoulder.

"Thank you for my cupcake."

"Yes, thank you. You are a blessing to our family, dishing out encouragement with your wonderful cupcakes." She smiled and dropped a bill in Livvy's brightly decorated tip jar before gently touching Abbie's dark braids. "We best be getting out of Miss Livvy's way. She's going to have customers lined up around the block if we don't get moving."

The pair started to move from their place in front of the truck before Abbie's mom stopped and laid a hand on Livvy's. "One more thing before we go. I reckon you've got some thinking and praying to do about that television show. Just remember to keep the thinking and the praying in the proper order."

"Thank you." Livvy nodded and gave Abbie a final wave before the girl went skipping down the sidewalk in front of her mother. She sighed at the empty concrete directly in front of her truck. If only the line around the block was a real problem. As the pair were turning the corner, Livvy spied the bill in her tip jar—more than enough to cover the cupcake. God always provided.

Could she really complain? Each week brought enough customers and special orders to make her payment to the bank on time and in full. She even had enough to live on. But it would be wonderful to have a little extra each month to tuck away in savings for a rainy day. Maybe *Cake That* was the answer.

A tap on her forehead jolted her back to the present. "Hello? Earth to Livvy."

She swatted Tabitha's hand away. "Do you mind? I was thinking."

"I could tell." Tabitha rolled her eyes. "So, are you going to do it?"

"Do what?"

"You know what? You're lucky I'm a pretty laid-back girl. No one else would put up with you."

"Fine. I want to pray about it tonight, but unless God tells me otherwise, I think I'm going to do it." She pushed her way past her friend in the tight space. "Now, if you'll kindly take your seat, I have special orders to complete while I wait for the afternoon rush."

2

Tabitha secured tape over the cardboard box they'd already filled. "I'd forgotten how much fun packing is. Reminds me why I don't go anywhere."

Livvy smirked as she stood by the closet, trying to figure out which items should fill the second box. "Hey, I was finishing breakfast while you were still snoring in the other room."

A pillow came out of nowhere. Livvy barely had time to swat it away before it hit her square in the face.

"I do not snore."

"Believe me, you do. As co-inhabitant of this house, I have had many opportunities to marvel at your nasal talents."

"You are no picnic either, I'll have you know. You use all the hot water every time you shower and can't cook a decent meal to save your life. Who would have thought a competitor on *Cake That* would fall apart completely when she has to do anything in the kitchen besides bake?"

Livvy's kitchen failures were no secret. Within two weeks of living together, they had agreed to modify their cooking arrangement. Desserts and breakfasts were her domain, but Tabitha did the heavy lifting for dinner. If the other bakers on *Cake That* ever found out her secret, she'd be laughed off the set.

"I can't believe it's here already." Livvy pushed an apron draped hanger out of the way. "I'm probably going to die of embarrassment, but who cares? I'll be on television."

"You have to take this one." Tabitha reached into the closet and removed a retro-inspired apron. "It's my favorite." The subtle brown, aqua, and white pinstriped material sported a ruffle of brown with white polka dots along the top and bottom edges. The same material created the apron's deep pockets and contrasted perfectly with the simple aqua ribbons that tied around the waist.

"I wouldn't dream of leaving it behind." Livvy took the apron and folded it neatly into the cardboard box sitting on the edge of her bed. "Can you rummage through my top drawer to find the matching headband while I keep looking?"

While her friend sifted through a drawer full of headbands that coordinated with her collection of aprons, Livvy pulled a red and white polka-dotted apron out of the closet. Its sweetheart neckline was trimmed with a tiny ruffle of cotton, and the waist tied with a simple white bow.

"While you're at it, grab the red and white headband that matches this one." She paused mid-fold. "You don't think it's too many polka dots, do you?"

Tabitha laughed as she continued to sift through the endless tangle of material in the drawer. "You're in trouble if too many polka dots is against their dress code. I think that's ninety percent of what you've got in there."

"I'm a polka dot girl." Livvy shrugged. "What can I say? They're too cute."

"They do garner attention." Tabitha's brows raised as she shook her head. "That's for sure. So, I think I'll stick with something a little more sedate."

"You need to live a little." Livvy plucked a black and white headband from the drawer and held it up to Tabitha's long blonde hair.

"Please." Tabitha snatched the band from Livvy's grasp. "I

live just fine, thank you. I'm simply not the life of the party like you are."

"Don't put that back." She giggled as she retrieved the band from Tabitha. "I think I'm going to take the matching apron with the purple trim and bow. With the ones I packed last night, I'll have ten sets. That's one for each episode of the show. Is it too much?"

"For me? Yes. For you? Absolutely not. They choose people with personality, and you have it to spare. The audience and judges are going to fall in love with you."

Livvy struck a superwoman pose, with fists on her hips and head held high. "What's not to love?"

She laughed as Tabitha rolled her eyes at the theatrics. Tabitha's mom always said they were as different as night and day, but they brought out the best in each other. Too bad she couldn't take Tabitha with her to the show. A tendril of fear spiraled through her.

"What if I don't win?"

"Don't start that again." Tabitha ran the packing tape over the box to secure the flaps. "You're good enough to win, Livvy."

"But what if I don't? I know the show is taping during the slow season, but I usually still have orders for customers' holiday events. It pays the bills when people don't want to stand in the cold for a cupcake. If I don't win, the truck—"

"You are going to do great." Tabitha placed a hand on each of her shoulders, making Livvy look her in the eye. "I can't promise you'll win, but I think you will. You're the best. Besides, God knows what you need. He'll take care of it."

"I know. You're right. I've got to stop worrying about this. I prayed about it before I sent in the audition tape. I prayed about it before accepting. Now, I've got to trust. I only wish it were easier."

Tabitha's eyes shut, and Livvy followed suit. A prayer was coming. Her friend was a prayer warrior like no one she'd ever met. Livvy might be the life of the party in their friendship, but Tabitha was the anchor that held them steady.

"Lord, be with Livvy on this new adventure. Help her do her best and be a light to those she meets. Let her compete with grace and confidence in the abilities You've given her. No matter what the outcome, let her know without a doubt that You're in control and taking care of her. You've laid out the path she's to take, and You will continue to do so after the show ends. Grow her and bless her through this opportunity. In Jesus' name, Amen."

Peace settled over Livvy. She could almost see her friend's prayer lifting to the throne room of heaven, where God caught it to Himself. Livvy offered her own silent prayer of thanks for giving her a friend as strong in her faith as Tabitha. Before the amen, she added a quick prayer asking God to grow the same kind of faith in her own life.

"Better?"

"Yeah. Much better. Thank you." Livvy smiled and glanced at the clock on her wall. "But now, I've got to get going. Are you sure you don't mind taking my boxes to the post office for me?"

"It's not a problem. You worry about being careful on the drive out to California. I'll make sure your clothes and stuff are waiting at your home away from home when you get there."

Livvy pulled her in for a tight hug. "You're the best."

"I know." Tabitha pulled away, placed a dramatic hand to her chest, and rolled her eyes. "Who could compare? Now get out of here, or you won't have time to sightsee on your trek across the country."

She couldn't stop the smile stretching across her face as she grabbed her keys and a mint green helmet from her nightstand before waving goodbye one last time. "Here goes nothing."

EVAN JONES SHUT the door to his truck without taking his eyes from the house in front of him. Was he in the right place? While by L.A. standards it might be average, it made the small Texan ranch house he'd grown up in look pathetic.

Everything he'd received to prep for his time on *Cake That* mentioned he'd live in a house with the other contestants, but nothing had prepared him for a mansion. He lifted his duffle bags from the truck bed. Before he could start up the walk, a motorcycle roared to a stop next to him.

The greeting he meant to offer his fellow competitor stuck in his throat as he turned to find a woman pulling a light green helmet from her head. Dark brown hair danced just below her shoulders, shimmering like silk in the California sun as she ran her fingers through it. A single lock of teal framed her face, deepening brown eyes which lit up as she turned to smile at him. Not what he'd expected, but a beautiful surprise.

"Hi. I'm Livvy."

The duffel bags he carried prevented Evan from immediately taking her offered hand. He dropped some of his load onto the sidewalk and shook her hand before picking it back up.

"I'm Evan." He hoped his smile was as open as hers and that his surprise didn't show on his face.

"Is it just me, or is this place a little daunting?" She motioned to the house with a tilt of her head. "I mean, it's beautiful, but I've never seen a house this big, at least not up close or intending to stay awhile."

He followed the direction of her gaze. Enormous copper framed windows stood out against the much lighter tan of the stone walls that rose to three stories, though one was sunk below street level at the front of the house. A multi-car garage sat at the south end of the home, and a chimney rose from the gray slate roof. The fireplace inside would set a mood more than fill a need.

Terraced garden plots followed the sloping stairway that led to the front door framed in large windows. In homage to the

California sun, a large bay window was positioned to the left of the entrance.

The front door opened, and a slim woman made her way toward them. Even hurrying down the walk, her movement reminded Evan of royalty or one of the women on the beauty pageant shows his momma liked to watch. Each step was designed to give the appearance of grace and beauty, though the straight set of her shoulders and intense expression told him she was used to taking charge.

"Apparently, in California, people don't walk." Livvy leaned in next to him, her voice meant only for him. "They glide. Do you think we'll all be gliding after a couple of weeks, or maybe you have to be a local?"

The woman drew closer, and Livvy forced a bland expression. Only a hint of her good humor remained in the upturned corner of her lips. He couldn't shake the feeling that Livvy was going to liven things up in this competition or erase his smile at the thought.

"You two must be Evan and Livvy." The woman's saccharin voice sounded forced as she clasped her hands in front of her chest. "I'm so glad you made it safely. I'm Rhonda, one of the production assistants on *Cake That*, and I've been charged with getting all our wonderful contestants settled."

A pause was usually an opening for others to speak, but Evan had the distinct impression this moment was nothing more than trained politeness. He waited for her to continue.

"Before you go in, I need to give you some instructions. A camera crew is inside the door. Don't look at them. Look at the house. Take in everything you can about the home. We need these reaction shots to splice together with other interactions away from the competition. The other contestants are waiting in the den. Join them for a few minutes, and then get your room assignments and get settled in. Got it?"

Evan saw Livvy look at him from the corner of his eye. He gave her a nod and shrug.

"It sounds great." Livvy turned a brilliant smile on their host. "I can't wait to meet everyone."

"Perfect. Right this way." Rhonda led them into a large entryway before turning to the left and waving them through an arched doorway. She gave a final reminder as they moved past her into the room. "Don't be shy. Go in and introduce yourselves to the other contestants. And most of all, don't watch the cameras."

3

Livvy felt Evan's presence beside her as they walked up the path to the front door, though she had a feeling he shortened his stride to allow her to keep up without jogging. At five feet, eight inches, she'd never been short. But Evan had to be at least six-four. And gorgeous, too.

Though she thought she'd covered it well, she had nearly been rendered mute when he turned his hazel-gray eyes on her. Of course, who retained their ability to speak in front of someone with the presence of a Hollywood leading man?

Honey-blonde curls flipped out from under his hunter-green beanie, and the matching scruff on his cheeks only added to the appeal. And when he smiled at her with those boy-next-door dimples? It was a wonder she could introduce herself at all. She only hoped she hadn't rambled incoherently.

"After you." He stepped in front of her to open the door and wave her inside.

She reminded herself to breathe. "Thank you."

What was wrong with her? She'd never reacted to a man like this, at least not to one who wasn't trapped on the silver screen. Her musings ended abruptly as she and Evan entered the den.

Plush sofas and chairs were arranged to create a perfect

sitting area. Everything was of the highest quality. One chair alone probably cost more than her entire apartment full of second-hand, yard sale furniture. An ornate brass chandelier would have bathed the room in a soft glow had the other lights been turned off. The room itself was more spacious than most of her apartment put together. Everything angled toward a massive fireplace that served as the focal point of the room.

The home she'd grown up in had a fireplace. She'd always liked its creek rock front and simple maple mantelpiece. It was practical and cozy. And compared to this one, it was plain. Larger than her bathroom at home, it was double-sided and encased in what looked like marble. Chic, sleek, and completely cold. Of course, what could you expect in a town where temperatures rarely dropped below the high forties? Why even have a fireplace?

Livvy licked her lips and hoped her discomfort wasn't evident on her face. It wouldn't do to have the first image of her on national television be that of a country bumpkin with her mouth gaped open like a fish. She needed to inspire confidence in the audience and judges. While the judges decided who moved on to the next round, audience perception could make or break a contestant after the show aired.

Eight pairs of eyes sized her up from their positions in the chairs arranged throughout the room. And that didn't include the ones hiding behind the cameras she wasn't supposed to look at, strategically placed in out-of-the-way corners. Well, waiting would only make the silence more awkward for everyone. It was time to let the competition know who she was and let them make up their minds about her. Livvy brushed a teal-streaked lock of hair from her face, straightened her shoulders, and smiled. Hopefully, she radiated warm and friendly rather than terrified and crazy.

Please, Lord, let me get along with at least some of my housemates.

"Hi, everybody. I'm Livvy Miller from St. Louis, Missouri, and I own a cupcake truck called The Sugar Cube."

Silence continued. She fidgeted. Why wasn't anyone speaking? Could it have something to do with the fact that her introduction sounded like a mid-year transplant into a new school? She nudged Evan with her elbow.

"And I'm Evan Jones."

He moved to take a seat. Livvy followed his lead and claimed one to the right of the fireplace. Gazes bounced between her and Evan. Not usually one without something to say, Livvy wasn't sure what to make of this group. After a few seconds that seemed like years, an older woman with fluffy white chin-length hair and slim shoulders smiled.

"I'm Genevieve. I've studied pastry in Paris, Switzerland, essentially everywhere you can find the most delectable sweets. It's a pleasure to meet you, Livvy and Evan."

Whoa. Did everyone have such a spectacular baking pedigree? Why in the world had the producers picked her as a contestant? Was she the weak link they expected to vote off in the first episode?

Hopefully, her nervous thoughts didn't translate into her expression. She nodded toward Genevieve and shifted in her seat. A tall, middle-aged man with an angular face and pointed nose as slender as his build dipped his head toward her. A shock of straight black hair fell into his face before he brushed it back.

"I'm Elliott. I have also trained under the best pastry chefs the world has to offer, though I call London my home." His accent was smooth and cultured, and despite the air of sophistication that hinted the man would be no fun, Livvy enjoyed the sound of his voice.

Her smile relaxed, though the fear of being the only non-classically trained pastry chef was growing with each introduction. "I'm glad to meet you."

A man who appeared closer to her age than any of the other male contestants, except maybe Evan, stood and crossed the room. His thick golden hair was combed back to highlight clear blue eyes. He extended a hand toward her and smiled.

"And you and I definitely need to get to know each other. I'm Will. And while I have the same high credentials, my experience came in the current century. But don't worry, honey. I'll be happy to share some of the tips and tricks you may have missed working in your little cupcake truck."

Livvy shifted uncomfortably and glanced at the other contestants. It had to be a misunderstanding; the man couldn't be as arrogantly insulting as she thought. Genevieve wouldn't look at her, and Elliot's smile seemed tight. Others fidgeted in their seats. Apparently, he could be as full of himself as he sounded. She returned her attention to him.

With as much politeness as she could muster, she shook his hand. "Good to meet you, Will."

He backed away, nodding as if he'd just given her the greatest privilege of her life. *Lord, are they all going to be like this? Please, let there be someone I can relate to.*

"I'm sure that offer to help would extend to anyone in the competition." Evan's easy voice cut through the tension. "Am I right?"

A sigh of relief escaped her lips as everyone's attention moved from her to Evan. Maybe God was going to provide a friend she could relate to after all. And if he distracted Will, that was even better.

"Evan, is it? And what's your training? I believe you omitted that from your introduction." Arrogance and disdain oozed from Will. His tone implied he thought Evan lower than dog mess on the bottom of a sneaker.

Evan remained unruffled under the group's scrutiny. In fact, stretched out in his chair, he looked beyond anyone's ability to bother. "I'm from Texas, and I—"

"Texas?" Will's chuckle as he interrupted was laced with derision. "Shouldn't you be on a barbeque competition show? I think you'll be out of your element here."

Frustration welled up in her as Will spoke. After only a few minutes, he was already getting on her nerves. This didn't bode well for the competition.

Evan simply shrugged.

"Not at all. My dad was the king of barbeque at our house, Mama ruled the kitchen, and Gram was the queen of baking. From the time I was a little squirt, I loved to help her with pies and cakes and anything else she happened to make." As he spoke of home and family, a bit of a drawl snuck into his voice.

Livvy grinned at the sound. If he wanted to keep talking about his Southern home, she wouldn't complain.

"So, you lack formal training?" Elliott inserted himself into the conversation.

Evan threaded his fingers together and leaned his head against them where they rested on the back of the chair. "Not at all. Home's what first lit that fire in me, but I've spent plenty of time building my knowledge of baking and honing my skills in the kitchen."

From the corner where he'd been sitting quietly, a man who appeared to be the oldest of the male competitors spoke up, both his voice and lightly olive-tinted skin hinting at Hispanic heritage. "Formal training is not the be-all, end-all. Perhaps of all sciences, ours has the distinction of being steeped in heritage, passed from one generation to the next. Talent existed long before degrees and certificates."

"Nicholas, please." Elliott rolled his eyes. "Years of culinary training under the best chefs cannot be overlooked in favor of training with a Nana in the home."

"And," Will cut in, "training from years ago cannot compare to what one currently receives. Think of all the advances in techniques that weren't available even thirty years ago."

Were they trying to bait him? As Livvy cringed at the insulting implication, Nicholas simply smiled at the pair. She tried to guess his age, but his round face and thick brown hair belied the salt and pepper in his trim beard and mustache. And though lines appeared around his eyes when he smiled, youthful dimples accompanied them.

The fifth male contestant cleared his throat. He adjusted plastic-framed glasses a few shades lighter than his skin's rich brown before speaking. "I believe, gentlemen, that there is merit in each style of learning the art, craft, and science of baking. I've known excellent pastry chefs from each camp. I've also seen them secure enough in their abilities to defend their own path without venom."

"Come now, David." Genevieve rolled her eyes. "You surprise me. Where's your defense of your macho male ego? Why don't you feel the need to mark your territory as the expert-in-residence like the others?"

"Not all men feel the need to prove themselves the bigger man." David speared her with a glance. "I suggest the results will speak for themselves as the competition progresses."

Genevieve opened her mouth to retort.

"I think what we need is a new start." A soft, easy voice came from a woman with porcelain skin and straight, dark hair. "Maybe we should go find out who our roommates are for the duration of the competition. We can get settled and be back down here by seven. That's when Rhonda said dinner will be served. Tonight, it's their treat. After that, we'll be on our own."

The woman who spoke looked about Livvy's height but carried a little more weight. Her round face was open and friendly. Livvy hadn't caught her name, but she was right. This battle of the egos would not lead anywhere good.

Livvy nodded in agreement. "I think that's wise. But I missed your name?"

The woman's smile seemed genuine. "I'm Harper. Emma's over there." She gestured to a slim blonde woman across the room before introducing the woman sitting next to Emma. "And this is Alyssa."

"Nice to meet you both." Livvy acknowledged the women with a smile.

While Emma could be described as cute or even pretty, Alyssa's warm caramel skin tone and wavy light brown hair could only be described as beautiful. Livvy would have guessed her a model instead of a baker.

Livvy stood and motioned her head toward the doorway. "Let's go find our roommates and explore this mansion before supper."

They stood almost as one and moved to the door. Some of the men continued to stare each other down, but others also began drifting away. Livvy watched Evan rise casually from his seat, as uninterested in the men's discussion as David.

Evan's gaze shifted to meet hers, and she jerked her eyes away. Her cheeks heated at having been caught. She scurried out the door behind the other women without another look back.

EVAN THOUGHT Livvy looked adorable with a blush blanketing her cheeks. There was a boldness in her lock of aqua hair and choice to ride a motorcycle cross-country for a baking competition, but she also blushed when caught looking at a guy from across the room. It was a unique combination.

Was her extroverted nature a show, or did she simply lack confidence around men? Evan had a feeling it would be worth the trouble to find out.

The uneasy feeling of negative attention came over Evan. He scanned the room. Will's narrowed eyes and rigid stance sent his arrogant alpha male message clearly without speaking a word. No trespassing.

The guy was delusional if he thought his brief, awkward exchange with Livvy meant anything. Livvy was polite, but it didn't take a genius to realize she had not been impressed. Evan lifted his chin in subtle defiance before following David from the room. Let Will interpret it how he wanted. If it made him think twice about approaching Livvy, good.

No one deserved a guy like Will, even if Evan didn't have plans to pursue her for himself. He was here to win *Cake That*. His family was counting on him, and that meant staying focused on baking instead of solving the mystery of Livvy, no matter how beautifully she blushed.

"THIS IS SO EXCITING. The drama's already starting! Did you see the way the guys were acting? This season is going to be the best!" Blonde and perky, Emma bounced up the stairs ahead of the group.

If the model of the group was Alyssa, Emma could, without question, fill the role of cheerleader. There were so many personalities filling the rooms of the house. Livvy took a deep breath. How much would their different styles play a part in how the competition panned out?

"I don't think grade school antics to determine the alpha are something we should be happy about, Emma." Alyssa shook her head as she followed at a more controlled pace.

The group unexpectedly stopped on the stairs, causing Livvy to bump into Genevieve. She looked up to find Emma facing the rest of the group with a pout.

"Well, I think you're wrong, Alyssa. I think it makes for great television and higher ratings. You agree with me, don't you, Harper?"

Harper bit her bottom lip, bouncing her attention from Emma to Alyssa and back again. "Personally, I don't like the added drama, but I can see your point about getting more viewers."

While this was not a full endorsement of her views, Emma smiled brightly and continued up the stairs to the first bedroom. The squeal she emitted as she read the names on the door was enough to make Livvy's eye twitch.

"I'm so glad we're getting the double room instead of the

triple. And have you seen the bathroom in this one? It's positively amazing!"

The cheerleader act would get old quickly if Livvy ended up on the list as Emma's roommate. Only she didn't believe it was an act. Emma took to it far too easily as she squealed again and grabbed Alyssa by the wrist.

Delicately removing her arm from Emma's grasp, Alyssa pushed a light brown curl away from her face. She smiled politely, but it didn't reach her dark brown eyes. Livvy could only imagine the thoughts going through Alyssa's head after the stairway conversation, but Emma didn't seem to think anything of it at all.

Another pout pushed Emma's lips out like a petulant toddler as she huffed. "Oh, come on, Alyssa. You know we're going to have a blast. It will be just like a sleepover in high school."

Though she wouldn't dare ask and confirm her suspicions, Livvy judged the pair to be several years older than her. The idea that someone in her early thirties could still act like Emma made her cringe. She hoped her feelings didn't show on her face. Alyssa said something too quiet to hear and followed her exuberant roommate into their new room.

Genevieve looked between Livvy and Harper. "Well, I guess that means the three of us will be sharing a room. Why don't we find it and get settled? Come along, Livvy, Harper."

With her theatrics, nobody would forget Emma soon. Harper and Genevieve would be easy enough to remember, too, since they were sharing a room. Now, if Livvy could manage to remember everyone else's names, she'd be set.

As Genevieve led them into the master bedroom, Livvy's mouth dropped open. No, her room at home was a bedroom. This couldn't be called anything but a suite. A bay window occupied the expanse of the outside wall, complete with a cushioned window seat to look out over the manicured lawn, pool house, hot tub, and pool.

Two full beds dominated one wall while a third sat against

the wall nearer the entrance. The three beds took up most of the floor space but still allowed glimpses of the plush rugs in muted whites, beiges, and blues covering the hardwood floor. Hopefully, they would have a place for all their belongings.

"Oh, my goodness." Harper's voice was full of awe as it echoed from the doorway on the opposite side of the room.

Livvy followed the voice into an alcove with a built-in vanity and mirror. "Harper?"

"I'm in here."

A right turn took Livvy in the correct direction. She looked in the first doorway on her left, but the only thing in that room was a toilet. A glance into a room on the right revealed a walk-in shower as big as her bathroom. She walked straight past both rooms into the most extravagant walk-in closet she'd ever seen. Built-in cherry wood shelves, racks, and drawers lined all the walls. A pale yellow granite island jutted out from one wall with more drawers underneath the countertop.

Taking it all in stride, Genevieve entered behind Livvy. "If you think this is nice, you should see our bathroom. Very posh."

Livvy and Harper waited only until she'd moved from the doorway before bolting out the door and across the short hall. An enormous tub, surrounded by the same yellow granite, waited to relax away the tensions of each day. Double sinks rested inside granite countertops over cherry drawers and cabinets.

The stone floor would be cold on bare feet if not for the plush white rugs scattered strategically throughout the narrow room. Above the tub were several small windows, high enough to avoid indecency and spaced often enough to provide natural light.

A sigh escaped Livvy's lips. Did she even really have to compete? Couldn't she spend her days relaxing with a good book in this gorgeous bathroom?

"I know, right?" Harper seemed to read her thoughts as she stepped in beside her. "And did you see the pool? Gorgeous. I mean, I know the network uses this house for all their reality shows and to house the competitors on shows like *Cake That*, but really. How are we supposed to focus with such luxury waiting for us?"

Livvy felt Genevieve's presence behind them.

"You focus because the luxury goes away the minute you get eliminated from the competition."

There was a little bit of Harper's romantic dreamer in Livvy, but she had a good dose of Genevieve's practicality too. Of course, she didn't have Genevieve's pedigree of top pastry chef instruction, but she hoped that wouldn't be an issue.

Both women seemed friendly enough that this arrangement just might work out perfectly. It could be worse. She could have to live in an unending slumber party with the cheerleader. Livvy was outgoing, but she'd never been considered bubbly. Squeals and over-the-top exuberance would get old fast.

4

L ivvy and the other nine contestants were shuttled to the studio lot early the next morning. *Cake That* was filmed in what appeared to be a warehouse from the outside. Before anything else, the contestants were herded through industrial-looking hallways for hair and makeup.

After a thorough conference room meeting expounding on all the rules and things to remember, Daniel, one of the production assistants, led them down one last hallway. This one was far more inviting, painted in bright colors with the *Cake That* logo emblazoned on the wall across from double electronic metal doors.

"Good morning." Rhonda stood at the edge of the doorway.

Her voice was too cheery to be natural this early in the morning. To reach that level of perkiness, Livvy would need a healthy dose of caffeine or a pain reliever by the afternoon. It was too over-the-top for her liking, but it suited what she'd seen of Rhonda so far.

The quick once-over she gave the group left Livvy feeling judged before the competition even started. She didn't have long to wait before finding out the verdict.

"You look great today. I've been asked to remind everyone all cell phones, tablets, or other internet-equipped devices are not allowed on set. If you have any of these items, please turn them in to Danny before walking through the door."

"It's Daniel."

A wave of her hand dismissed his concern. "Whatever. Give your items to Daniel."

Lips pressed flat, Daniel ran a hand through his unruly mop of wavy blonde hair. His shoulders rose and fell with a sharp intake of breath.

Livvy looked back to Rhonda flashing that too-sweet smile at the contestants. Did she realize how condescending she sounded? Low-level assistant or not, he was still a person. His frustration was evident, but Rhonda seemed oblivious to it.

When Daniel glanced her way, Livvy smiled sympathetically. Did his head dip slightly in acknowledgment, or was it wishful thinking?

The doors slid open. The nerves she'd battled since arriving tied her insides in knots. From her place at the back of the pack, Livvy heard gasps from other contestants before she got a complete look for herself. Her gasp added to the chorus as the full kitchen came into view. Though she'd seen it in the previous season, it took her breath away. Would this show ever stop surprising her?

The competition arena was huge. Every stainless steel and polished wood surface gleamed under the studio lighting. Ten perfectly ordered and expertly stocked workspaces were arranged on the main floor of the room. Each competitor would have ample space to complete their daily tasks.

A community pantry and walk-in refrigerator were visible through a glass wall to the left of the door they'd just entered. Two walls lined with blast chillers and convection ovens made up the outside edges of the baking area. Bright colors and playful designs filled the otherwise unoccupied spaces.

A wide raised platform held the judges' table and contestants' viewing area on the far end of the room. From this refuge, those declared safe each episode would watch the two lowest-ranked competitors duke it out for one last opportunity to wow the judges.

And there they were. The two permanent judges sat behind their table with knowing smiles. Livvy sucked in a deep breath. The idea of having them judge her ability was one thing; the reality of it was unnerving.

Waves of confidence poured off Taylor Prince. It wasn't arrogance. It was the knowledge that he was on top in the world of cake decorating. Liberal golden highlights were visible in the long brown hair he wore combed to the left over razor-short sides.

To Livvy, it screamed of a man fighting to retain his youth in the face of middle age, but no one ever found fault with him. He was quick to laugh and as down to earth as anyone, if tabloids could be believed.

Adeline Li's smile was a little more reserved but still made its way to her eyes. Livvy couldn't imagine how she would bake with the sweeping black bangs of her chin-length bob making a curtain in front of her eyes, but Adeline was a pro. She and her bakery had been the star of their own show, *Adeline Li's Little Bites*, before joining the *Cake That* judges' table. Livvy had watched it a few times, and though it wasn't full of the energy Taylor exuded, anyone could tell Adeline knew her stuff.

Before she realized what was happening, Livvy found herself standing before the judges with the rest of the competitors. It was all so surreal. She'd need at least a year after getting home to process everything properly.

"He's really not all that important, you know. Everyone thinks he's a great expert, but he hasn't even had the same kind of in-depth training I have." Will's whisper in her direction dropped her firmly back into reality.

Why did he have to keep talking? No, that wasn't fair. Love everyone. She was supposed to love everyone. Even the annoying ones. Okay, she'd have to try extra hard with Will. There had to be some redeeming quality to the man.

For now, he was standing too close. Inching away from Will, Livvy brushed arms with Evan. He smiled down at her and scooted over to make room. Did he think she'd done it on purpose? Livvy licked her lips. Not that she'd be so coy, but he couldn't know that.

Taylor's voice from the table in front of her broke through her private monologue. Great. He'd been speaking, and she hadn't paid a bit of attention. She better get herself under control, or she'd lose before she even had a chance to compete.

"So, our first challenge is a nod to where our filming this season takes place. You have four hours to complete a trio of cupcakes and one fully decorated cake that honors California. And your time begins now."

The idea for her cake came immediately. Livvy joined the other competitors as they raced to their stations. She quickly did a rough sketch of the finished design and headed to the pantry. Several contestants were filling up their baskets with citrus and wines. She headed straight for cocoa, almonds, and marshmallows. As certain as she was no one would have a cake like hers, she was equally skeptical whether or not the judges would appreciate her take on California.

Time flew as Livvy and the others mixed up their batters. She filled her pans and stepped back from the counter.

"Behind you."

Livvy paused as Alyssa raced behind her to the ovens. She checked both ways before moving that direction herself. With her cake pans in the oven, she went to work preparing the muffin tins for the cupcakes. As soon as her cakes were done, the cupcakes would bake while she cooled and began decorating the main cake.

Pans clattered against the tile floor. Livvy jumped at the unexpected noise. Emma glared at Will, her empty hands spread out in front of her. Will's held a cake pan and a muffin tin. It had to be Emma's cake on the floor.

"You did that on purpose! What am I going to do now? I don't have time to redo my cake and get it decorated too."

Livvy cringed. No voice should hold that much whine, even under conditions as stressful as these.

"Not my problem." Will shrugged. "You need to watch where you're going."

"You should have said you were behind me."

"That's not an actual rule, you know."

"I don't care. It's what people do. It tells them there is someone they need to watch out for. You've ruined my chances."

Did Livvy have time to help? She glanced at the clock before taking stock of her workstation. Her cakes were cooling on the counter. She had already made the frosting and gotten her cupcakes in the oven. She made her way to Emma's station.

"Emma, you don't have time to argue with him. Come on. Tell me what you need, and I'll help you get a new batch mixed up." Livvy tugged on Emma's sleeve when she hesitated.

"It's no use." Emma reluctantly followed. "I'm done."

With a hand on each of Emma's shoulders, Livvy looked her straight in the eyes. "Stop it, Emma. You can at least get something plated for the judges. Now, tell me what to do."

Emma sucked in her bottom lip and wiped the tears from under her eyes. She inhaled a shuddering breath before regaining her composure enough to speak. "Can you zest some oranges for me while I get the batter put together?"

The pair flew into action. Livvy knew precisely how much time she had until her cupcakes were ready to come out of the oven. When she glanced toward the countdown clock, she noticed Nicholas standing next to Emma. He nodded at her instructions before moving to clean out and prepare the pans for the new batter.

Good. Maybe this year's competition wouldn't be as cutthroat as some cooking shows she had seen.

"You guys are wasting your time. She's not going to have anything done, and now you won't either." Will was undoubtedly going to be the thorn in her side where keeping a godly attitude was concerned.

Livvy refused to comment. As she scooped the zest into a prep bowl and placed it beside Emma, she said a silent prayer for patience.

"Here's the zest. You've got this." She squeezed Emma's shoulder before moving to the ovens to retrieve her cupcakes. It was time she got back to work on her own creation.

Gingerly sprinkling finely ground almonds over her cupcakes, Livvy added the final touch as the buzzer sounded. The time she spent with Emma had cost her, but she'd still managed to finish. More than that, she'd done the right thing. Win or lose, she had every reason to be proud of her performance.

"Livvy. Please present your California creation."

Livvy smoothed her brown polka-dot apron, then lifted the display board for what seemed like an endless march to the judging table. Exuding confidence was difficult when simultaneously walking and balancing a heavy cake that could make or break your time in a competition. She straightened her shoulders, concentrated on keeping the board level, and finally remembered to breathe as she successfully slid her completed entry onto the judge's table.

The judges eyed her cake momentarily. Taylor's eyes narrowed as he glanced from the cake to her. "California was today's theme?"

She cleared her throat. "Yes, sir."

"And you've brought us something that looks very chocolate. I didn't see you use wine or typical California produce in this either. Can you tell us what you've made us today and why?"

Could they hate it already? They hadn't even tried it yet. She hoped her smile didn't resemble a grimace. But her nerves were wreaking havoc on her stomach, so she couldn't guarantee it.

"Today, I've made for you a dark chocolate cupcake and cake

with ground almonds. I used fluffy marshmallow frosting on the cupcakes and as the cake filling. I made the cake into a round scoop of rocky road ice cream and frosted it with chocolate marshmallow mixed with dollops of white marshmallow frosting. I used a torch to give a golden toasting to the frosting on the cupcakes, and I sprinkled ground almonds on top.

"I chose to honor rocky road ice cream because Oakland, California, was the birthplace of this classic ice cream flavor during the Depression. I hope you enjoy it." She clasped her hands in front of her, but quickly moved them behind her back to avoid fidgeting in front of the judges.

They had to know she was nervous, but it wouldn't do her any good to show it. Their expressions were unreadable. After a moment of silent eating and note-taking, they dismissed her to return to the group.

Each competitor went through the same process. Even Emma managed to get her citrus cake and cupcakes plated on time, though less creatively than she probably intended. Not once did the judges give any indication of their approval or dislike of anyone's offerings.

Adeline leaned toward Taylor and said something too quietly to be heard by the group. He nodded his head and pointed to his notes. Adeline nodded back and straightened.

"The following are safe from elimination today: Nicholas, Elliott, Alyssa, Harper, Evan, Will, and Genevieve. You may come sit in the viewing area."

A rock settled in Livvy's stomach as she watched the other competitors move away. A glance at Emma confirmed she was close to tears for the second time in the day's competition. David fidgeted beside her, but his eyes were on the judges. Livvy turned as well.

Taylor looked each of them in the eyes before continuing. "Emma, you had a disaster in the kitchen today, and it almost took you out of the competition completely. Without your fellow competitors stepping up to help, you might not have finished. What you brought to us was complete but sloppy. Your flavors were less than original, and your plating was dull."

"David," Adeline took over. "Your plating was excellent, but your flavors missed the mark. Your frosting was overly sweet and heavy. Your cake was on the edge of being overdone."

Training his eyes on Livvy, Taylor folded his hands in front of him. "Livvy, your flavors and plating were spot-on. Your cake was well done.

"It's your adherence to the theme we question. We were amazed to find out Rocky Road ice cream was invented in California, and therein lies the problem. We wanted cake flavors that encapsulated California, and without your background, we wouldn't have known. We applaud out-of-the-box thinking, but this time you may have moved too far out of the box."

"David, Emma, and Livvy—one of you will join the others in the viewing area. The other two will go back to their stations for the elimination round." Adeline punctuated her announcement with the raising of her chin.

The judges silently appraised the three contestants. Livvy swallowed hard, refusing to look anywhere but the judges' table in front of her.

"Emma, you are going to the elimination round." Adeline continued.

Breathing became more difficult as Livvy's chest tightened. She prayed she could hear Adeline's announcement over the sound of her heart beating and fought the urge to shift her weight from one foot to the other.

"Livvy, we applaud your creative take on the theme, but be judicious in how far you stray from the box. This time, your flavors, execution, and presentation were enough to save you. Please join the others in the viewing area."

She slapped her hand to her chest as if the weight of it would keep her thundering heart in its place. The desires to shout and cry waged war inside her, but one look at David brought her back to earth. He was going to the elimination round with

Emma. A twinge of guilt settled in; her success meant another's defeat.

"Great job, Livvy." David's smiled looked forced, but his congratulations sounded sincere.

"You're going to do fine." She laid a hand on his arm to offer some reassurance before he moved back into the challenge area with Emma. Only the tightness in his jaw betrayed his nerves, a stark contrast to Emma's lip-biting and uncontrollably blinking eyes. Livvy was sure the girl would have a total meltdown right on camera, but the judges were merciful in laying out the challenge without delay.

How could time stand still and yet pass so quickly? The elimination round seemed to creep by, yet, before they knew it, the judges had tasted their cakes and made a decision. David was safe, but Emma's time on the show was through.

Livvy moved with the rest of the group to shake David's hand and hug Emma goodbye. At the first sign of trouble, Emma had lost control of her emotions and broken down completely. What she'd managed to plate was sloppy and underbaked.

Though David deserved the win, Livvy couldn't help feeling for Emma. She didn't know Emma that well, but only those who were more than competent were chosen for the show. People might look back at her loss and consider her a poor baker when, really, she just couldn't handle pressure well. It had to be embarrassing.

"A blind man could have seen that one coming." Will's voice carried.

Why did he have to be so rude? Livvy cringed, hoping Emma didn't hear it.

"Do you have to be so unprofessional?" Genevieve huffed as she gave voice to what Livvy felt. "Emma is a fellow competitor, and she deserves our support."

Livvy shifted as Genevieve edged her way past to get away from Will.

"Don't know why she thinks so. Emma's obviously not the right caliber of baker," Will muttered.

If only she could get away from the man and his harsh words. Why couldn't Will be eliminated? Emma's cheerleader squeals were far easier to deal with than his conceit.

The remaining competitors made their way outside and climbed into the waiting SUVs, more than ready to return to the mansion. Livvy didn't expect Will to scoot in right beside her and couldn't help but hope that tomorrow might find him in the elimination round. She looked out the window. Hopefully, this would be the last time Livvy would find herself beside him for the rest of the competition.

5

"You don't stand a chance, you know? With the competition or Livvy." Will's voice broke the silence in the room. "Why don't you save yourself some embarrassment and bow out now?"

So much for a few minutes of rest before their pizza was delivered. Evan kept still on the bed, refusing to open his eyes. With everyone worn out from the day's competition, the decision to order dinner was unanimous, and to Evan, it seemed the perfect opportunity to decompress after a long day. He needed a little silence to reset before socializing with his housemates all evening.

"Don't think you're fooling me. I know you're not asleep."

"Can't you leave him alone? It's obvious he just wants to rest for a few minutes."

Evan fought a groan. He knew David was trying to stand up for his fellow competitor, but regardless of the reason, the results wouldn't be good.

"This doesn't concern you. Why don't you go study a cookbook? After today's elimination round, you could definitely use the help."

"That's enough, Will." Though he still didn't open his eyes,

Evan knew he had to step in. "David, would you mind checking to see if the pizza's here yet?"

"Sure. I'll come get you when it's here."

"You've got some nerve." Evan sat up, leveling Will with a look. "You come into our room, uninvited, and insult us? That's not right."

"Please," Will scoffed. "You know David doesn't matter in this competition. He'll be out of here before today's cakes have time to cool."

"Even if that were true, which it's not, it doesn't mean he isn't worth common decency."

Will waved the idea away. "Whatever. I only came in here to make sure you understand—I play to win. And right now, I plan on winning far more than the prize money at the end of the competition. Livvy may not be at my level of expertise when it comes to baking, but I'm sure she has many other worthwhile talents hidden in that beautiful package. And I intend to find out what they are before she's voted off the show. So stay out of my way."

The guy was disgusting. With each word he spoke, Evan felt his muscles tightening. The urge to get in his face was overwhelming, but he forced a deep breath.

"Get out."

A spark of something lit in Will's eyes before he schooled his features, shrugged one shoulder, and stalked from the room.

Evan sat on the edge of his bed, eyes closed, and forced several more deep breaths. If he let Will, or anyone else, get in his head, he could kiss winning goodbye. And that was why he was here.

A framed family photo sat on the nightstand by his bed. His parents stood behind him and his two sisters in the backyard of his childhood home. They were in love as much now as when the picture was taken during his high school graduation party.

The Jones family didn't have a lot in the way of things, no extra money for vacations or expensive gifts. What they had was each other, and Evan had never felt the void of what they couldn't provide. He'd had a great childhood, filled with loving memories, and his time on *Cake That* would be his way of returning the favor.

When he won, the winnings would go a long way in updating the Jones home and giving his parents the family vacation they'd always talked about but could never afford. Evan smiled as he thought about presenting the tickets to them as a surprise for their thirty-fifth wedding anniversary in the spring. It would be the perfect way to honor the two who'd been cheering him on for as long as he could remember.

"I cannot let Will get in my head," Evan reinforced the reminder by saying it out loud. "I don't need distractions to keep me from my goal."

And, contrary to what Will thought, he wasn't here to get a girl either. Even if she seemed as sweet as she was beautiful. He would enjoy getting to know Livvy better if the circumstances were different, but they were competitors. He needed it to stay that way to keep his focus and win the grand prize. He'd do whatever he could to keep her away from Will's unwanted attention, but friendship with Livvy was all he could afford to give.

LIVVY DROPPED onto one of the dining room chairs and reached for a slice of thin-crust ham with pineapple and jalapeños. She raised the slice of cheesy goodness to her lips.

"While I would normally argue against pineapple on pizza, I have to give you points for adding a little heat to it." Will's voice came from across the table. "I knew the first time we met you were a girl that liked a little spice in your life."

If she'd had any thoughts of continuing with her meal, they were abandoned upon seeing the glint in Will's eyes. Gross. Even lacking experience with men flirting, Livvy had the distinct impression that his attempts at flirtatious come-ons went beyond annoying and juvenile. Given any encouragement at all, she believed they'd escalate to inappropriate.

Deciding how to respond wasn't easy. Livvy stared at her plate. She had no desire to be mean, but she shouldn't have to put up with his behavior either. How could she make it stop without crossing the line into nastiness? She'd never been put in a position like this before. *Please, God, show me how to deal with him.*

The answer came in a deep voice with just a hint of a drawl. "I'm headed out to the patio to eat. Anyone want to join me?"

She glanced up and met Evan's eyes, which looked green more than gray now that he wore a T-shirt and his trademark beanie, both the color of an evergreen forest. If she'd had any doubts that his words were meant to give her an out, his quick wink and lopsided smirk would have dispelled them instantly. Would she ever get to eat? First, Will made her appetite flee in disgust. Now, a conspiratorial look from Evan set loose a million butterflies in her stomach.

"I think I'll join you." She stood, picking up her plate and glass. "We've been inside all day. Fresh air would do me good." She waited only until Evan filled his own plate before leading the way outside.

The covered stone patio was pleasantly shaded and looked out over a perfectly trimmed backyard, including numerous flower beds and an enormous above-ground pool. A hot tub dominated the space at one end of the patio, while a dining set with enough seating for all ten contestants took up residence on the other. Livvy sat in one of the cushioned chairs and placed her food on the glass tabletop.

"Thank you for rescuing me."

Evan's hair grazed his shoulder as he tipped his head to the side. "Who says I was rescuing you? Maybe I was protecting Will. I have a feeling he might have gotten a tongue lashing if I hadn't intervened."

The image made Livvy laugh. "I don't know how it happened, but he's been right beside me making arrogant remarks every time I turn around today. It's getting to be a little much, and I think they may even be getting close to inappropriate at times. I'm not sure how much longer praying for patience is going to work."

"You aren't sure how it happened?" His brows drew together. "Really?"

"What do you mean?"

"You really don't know?"

Clearly, she had missed something. Now, if she could figure out the tidbit of information he seemed to think was common knowledge, she'd be set.

"Oh no, have the producers told him to annoy me or something? Is he supposed to get under my skin and distract me from the competition?"

Evan smiled. Despite the distinct impression that he was attempting to avoid a laugh at her expense, Livvy returned it with one of her own. It couldn't be helped. Who could resist those dimples?

"He's everywhere you are because that's where he wants to be. He's attracted to you and trying his hardest to impress you. Only problem is, what must usually work for him is only irritating you."

The unladylike snort escaped before Livvy could stop it. Evan thought Will seriously liked her? Romantically? Ugh. While she'd dreamed of one day finding a man who wanted more than friendship with her, Will was not that guy. Besides, this was a show. It wasn't real.

"I think he just wants someone to feed his ego and make him the center of attention. It's a ploy for the cameras. Just for show."

She would have enjoyed Evan's laugh if it wasn't prompted by what she'd said.

"Of course, Will wants someone to do those things, but

he's chosen you as that person. He flaunts his ability with everyone. He puts everyone down – everyone but you. Even you said you noticed how he's always right beside or behind you."

"It's not real, though. He's doing it for the show."

"No, he's doing it for you. Trust me."

"I don't know."

"I do. You weren't looking at him when I interrupted you two. If looks could kill, he'd already be arrested and charged with murder. I'm guessing he's kicking himself right now for not offering the patio himself. I can guarantee he'd jump at the chance to have you to himself."

The patio door slid open. Harper paused when she saw them sitting at the table, and her cheeks colored pink. "I'm sorry. I didn't realize anyone was out here. I'll leave you two alone."

Heat crept into Livvy's face at the image Harper's words created in her mind. Might be nice, but it wasn't what Harper thought. Guys like Evan didn't see her that way. They never had.

"You're not interrupting anything." She smiled and motioned for Harper to sit. "Join us. We came outside for a place with ... a better atmosphere."

Evan's foot pushed out the chair opposite him. "That seat has your name on it."

With a glance over her shoulder, Harper considered the alternative. The right side of her bottom lip tucked between her teeth. Was she about to refuse?

"Join us. Evan and I would love the company."

"Are you sure?" She edged toward the empty seat.

A new person at the table might be what they needed to change the topic from Will. Livvy nodded. "We're positive."

"What did you think of today's competition?" Evan included Harper the moment she sat down.

"I felt horrible for Emma, and I hope she didn't hear Will's comments." Harper shrugged. "But I felt really sorry for Daniel too."

"Daniel?" Livvy thought through the day and all the people she'd met. "You mean the intern on the production crew?"

Conversation stalled momentarily as Harper finished her bite of pizza and took a drink. "I hated the way Rhonda dismissed him in front of everyone."

The day's events played through Livvy's mind as she searched for the one Harper referenced. There was a time when she felt a little bad for him, but it didn't seem like that big a deal. She couldn't even remember what prompted it, only the feeling. She looked to Evan. He shrugged and shook his head. They both turned to Harper.

"Daniel hates being called Dan or Danny or anything other than Daniel. It's too childish. He wants to be taken seriously. When she practically ignored his correction of his name like it wasn't worth her time, I don't know. It was just rude and uncalled for. It really bothered him."

That's what it was. But even with the details filled in, Livvy still didn't see why it affected Harper so much or how she'd know anything about how much it bothered Daniel. None of them had conversed with the production assistant beyond stage directions. Oh, she did recall seeing Harper standing close to him several times during breaks in filming. It was starting to make sense, but Harper needed to be careful.

Livvy shrugged, wanting to warn Harper without getting her defenses up. "I didn't talk to Daniel or anyone else on the crew all that much. I think hanging out with anyone other than the competitors is frowned on by the higher-ups. I try to keep my distance so I don't rock the boat."

"It's more a preference than a rule, I think, but thanks for the heads-up. Daniel is just fun to talk to, and he knows so much about the show. Did you know *Cake That* was actually his idea? If it does well, he won't be an intern for long."

The story sounded like a desperate attempt on Daniel's part to gain Harper's attention. Could Harper be that gullible? Evan's eyes reflected casual concern and more than a hint of doubt.

That wasn't encouraging. Livvy sipped her soda and considered her options. Harper was a grown woman who could make her own decisions, but Livvy hated to see her chances in the competition harmed because an intern wanted her attention.

The door opened, and the rest of the housemates spilled out onto the patio. If Harper's talk got around, they could make trouble for her. She would keep it quiet, and Evan didn't seem the gossipy type, but she couldn't say the same for the others.

"I wouldn't say anything about talking to Daniel with anyone else." Leaning close, she spoke only loud enough for Harper to hear. "It may be an unwritten rule, but other contestants could cry foul and create a bunch of drama. If they do, that could put you in a bad place in the competition. I don't want that for you."

Harper nodded. "Right. You've got a point. I'll keep it to myself, don't worry."

As Harper vacated her chair to join the others, Evan moved to claim it. When the group was close enough to the pool to be out of earshot, Evan spoke. "Were you warning her to be careful?"

"Yes. I hope she listens. What do you make of all Daniel's talk?"

"I think he's probably harmless, except for the damage it could do to Harper in the competition if anyone else catches wind of it."

A bead of sweat trailed down the outside of Livvy's glass. She swept it away. "But the stuff about coming up with *Cake That*. Do you think there's any truth in it?"

Evan grabbed her empty plate and deposited it with his in the covered trash can. When he looked back at her with a hint of a smile on his lips, excitement skittered through her.

"I think he's a man, trying to impress a woman he finds attractive."

Get a grip, girl. He's not talking about you. Her gaze darted to the pool. Evan was talking about Harper and Daniel. There was no underlying message in his words, no matter what her currently non-working lungs were trying to tell her. She cleared her throat.

"You're probably right. I only hope he doesn't get her into trouble."

"I'm sure Harper will be fine."

Livvy didn't argue. Only time would tell, but Livvy liked Harper and hoped for her sake Evan was right.

6

"Welcome back, contestants."

The judges began their instruction for the day's events while Livvy stood with the other contestants. This time, she'd managed to move at the last moment to stand beside Alyssa on the opposite side of the group from Will.

She leaned in close. "What do you think today's challenge is going to be?"

"From the judges?" Alyssa raised her eyebrows. "I'm sure we're about to find out. For you? Avoiding Will, if the goo-goo eyes from across the room are any indication."

Peering around Alyssa, Livvy's gaze collided with Will's. Great. Now he thought she was watching him back. When would she learn curiosity never worked in her favor? She returned her attention to Adeline's instructions.

"You'll find a covered dish at each of your stations. The ingredient at your station is your inspiration for today's creations. You must use this flavor in today's cake and cupcake. You have four hours, starting now."

Livvy rushed to her station and lifted the lid from her secret ingredient. Cinnamon disks. Her secret star of the show was cinnamon candy? In a cake and cupcakes?

A glance toward Genevieve's station next to her revealed honeycomb sitting on the silver tray in her workspace. A station farther, it looked like Will had gotten bacon. She didn't have time to check out what everyone else received. She had to figure out what she could do with cinnamon candy.

Too much of the main ingredient would render her offering inedible, but enough had to be present to leave no doubt she had stayed true to the flavor of the candy. Cinnamon and chocolate paired well together. But would it be too expected?

Livvy scribbled furiously on the pad of paper at her station as inspiration struck. Once she had a rough sketch, she grabbed her basket and headed to the pantry. Hopefully, she'd find everything she needed still there. A quick look around the room showed she was the last one to make it to the pantry.

As Livvy measured her dry ingredients into a bowl, Genevieve's voice cut into her concentration. "Do you still have the sugar, Will?"

Without even taking time to look up from his work, Will answered. "No. I used it and put it back. Left-hand side. Third shelf down from the top."

Glaring at his clipped tone, Genevieve moved behind him to retrieve the sugar. The space between Livvy and Will was now empty. He noticed the removal of the buffer between them at the same time she did.

"What are you working on over there? You seem to be concentrating awfully hard."

"I am." She refused to look at him. "I'd like to finish my cake on time and with all the right flavors."

"If you need any ideas, let me know. I've always excelled with flavor pairings."

She tightened her grip on the knife as she chopped apples. "I think I'll be okay."

A sigh escaped her lips when Genevieve stepped up to her station. With the much-appreciated barrier separating them, it would be easier to keep Will from derailing her concentration.

She had to give the judges something to wow them this time. Though she hadn't gone to the elimination round in the previous event, she'd been closer than she liked. Now she was racing the countdown clock—only an hour left to complete her cakes.

As nervous as the day before, Livvy made her way to the judging table. Her cake had turned out exactly as planned. She placed it on the table and stepped back.

"What I have for you today is an apple cake decorated as a candy apple. The icing is a cinnamon buttercream with a red cinnamon glaze for that candy apple shine, and the stick peeking out is a shortbread cookie. The cupcakes are the same apple cake with cinnamon buttercream. Instead of drizzling them with glaze, I melted cinnamon disks and topped the cupcakes with delicate candy shards. I hope you enjoy them both."

The judges seemed pleased as they took bites from both the cake and cupcakes. Of course, neither said anything, so it was impossible to know for sure. She smiled and nodded as she moved back into the group.

Will stepped forward with the swagger and arrogance she'd come to see as typical for him. He was rewarded with the wall of bland expressions that neither confirmed nor denied the excellence of the baked goods set before them. It didn't seem to rattle him. Livvy was sure the possibility that the judges wouldn't like his cakes never even crossed his mind.

David presented his cakes to the judges, seeming confident in his abilities but unsure of the judges' responses. Evan and Alyssa followed suit. None of the three radiated the same prideful attitude Will carried everywhere he went. Maybe—hopefully—today would be the day they could say goodbye to the arrogance once and for all. Then she wouldn't have to deal with him in the house, either. That would be nice.

The next to offer up her finished product was Genevieve. She set her perfectly decorated beehive-shaped cake on the table. Miniature fondant bees with glassy hard candy wings were poised just above the cupcakes' frosting and around the outer edge of the beehive cake. It looked amazing. Livvy had to admit, Genevieve had taken the baking-friendly ingredient and elevated it.

Adeline sputtered and covered her chest with one hand as the other fumbled for a napkin. As discreetly as possible, she emptied the contents of her mouth into it and continued to cough as she reached for some water.

"A bit dramatic today, Adeline? It can't be that bad. It's a honey cake." Taylor rolled his eyes and lifted a forkful to his lips.

As the cake hit his tongue, his eyes widened. He cleared his throat as he continued to chew. He looked to Adeline out of the corner of his eye, but she was staring at him with raised brows. Livvy could see the effort it took for him to swallow. He cleared his throat once again.

"I think I owe you an apology, Adeline."

Her terra cotta-glossed lips pursed. "You think?"

As she turned her attention to Genevieve, Livvy did the same. If she was shocked, she hid it well, standing perfectly still and straight with her chin raised high. Genevieve was almost the perfect picture of a poised lady. Only the slight widening of her eyes hinted at the storm of anxiety that must be churning inside her.

Movement at the judge's table drew Livvy's gaze.

"Genevieve, did you taste your cake at any time?" Adeline pushed her plate away.

"No. I did not." Her cultured voice was sure and strong. "I've made this honey walnut cake many times through the years. The recipe is as known to me as my own name."

Taylor nodded slowly. "Maybe you should have. This cake looks amazing, but it is completely inedible. I believe you have inadvertently switched out the sugar for salt."

Genevieve's mouth dropped open. All poise was lost. Her head whipped around toward the rest of the group, and if she could have called fire down from heaven, she would have directed it at Will.

"It was you! This is your doing!" Fury filled her voice.

"I don't know how you figure that." Will crossed his arms in front of his chest, meeting her stare without flinching. "I wasn't ever at your station. Seems to me you might need to pay more attention when you're baking."

Her eyes narrowed to slits. "I asked you where you put the sugar, and I took it from the exact spot in the pantry you indicated."

The bored expression on Will's face matched his matter-of-fact tone. "I hate to disappoint you, Genevieve, but I don't need to sabotage you to win this competition. Your outdated techniques and flavors—"

A heavy-handed slap of a palm against the judges' table broke into their argument. "All right, you two, enough." Taylor looked back and forth between Will and Genevieve. "We'll get to the bottom of this." He signaled toward some of the crew standing toward the back of the set. "Dan, can you check the pantry and let us know what you find?"

"Until we hear otherwise, we are going to proceed with the tasting and elimination round of competition." Adeline folded her hands together in front of her. "Barring confirmation of sabotage, Genevieve, you will be in the elimination round today. Please move to the side. We have three more cakes to judge."

Livvy's insides were tied in knots as she watched the remaining contestants step up to the judge's table. Sabotage? Would Will stoop to something so underhanded? Genevieve was a professional, but more than that, Livvy considered her a throwback to the old style of being a lady. Her explosion at Will seemed out of character. Genevieve must have been sure of what she said.

It only took a few moments for Daniel to return from the pantry. He stepped between Adeline and Taylor's seats and knelt. Their looks of concern and confusion were the only clues to what Daniel had found since none of the competitors could hear what was said.

Curt nods from the judges sent Daniel scurrying to his position at the back of the set. Adeline and Taylor continued to whisper between themselves for a moment longer before addressing the contestants.

"We had several great entries to choose from today," Adeline said. "I'm pleased to announce Livvy, Nicholas, Harper, Evan, David, and Elliott are all safe from elimination this week. Please take your places in our viewing area."

Livvy would have been relieved under normal circumstances, but now the decision barely took the edge off her nerves. What would happen to the others? She watched them from the safety of her seat.

Alyssa chewed her bottom lip with her hands clutched in front of her. Will and Genevieve stood on opposite sides of Alyssa. Her presence did nothing to deter the glares they shot at each other until Taylor spoke from the judges' table.

"Genevieve, we have already discussed the reason you're in elimination this week. Whether or not you were sabotaged makes no difference. Your cake today was inedible. Will, you are here because of your possible part in this predicament. If we determine you had a hand in sabotage, you will be automatically removed from the show."

A storm of emotion passed over the contestants' faces, but none had time to respond.

"However, Alyssa, your cake bordered on being too dry to enjoy," Taylor continued. "While your flavors were beautiful, your presentation was a little haphazard as well. If you're around after today's elimination round, I would suggest paying more attention to detail."

A polite smile from Adeline did nothing to put the trio at ease. Her gaze passed over all three of them before returning to land on Will. "In light of the claim of sabotage leveled against you, one of our staff has completed a thorough investigation of the pantry. Salt was indeed on the shelf you directed Genevieve to during the competition."

Will's mouth opened to argue, but at Adeline's raised hand, he shut it again. "As I was saying, the salt was there, but the sugar container was also on the shelf. They were right next to each other, and it is the decision of the judges and show producers there is no clear-cut evidence of sabotage. Will, you are free to join the others in the viewing area. Genevieve and Alyssa, you will compete in the elimination round."

Accepting her fate, Alyssa nodded. Her own work had landed her in her current position. Genevieve was another story. She continued to glare at Will, smugly seated in the viewing area.

When she turned to the judges, Livvy could only pray things weren't about to get ugly.

"I will not participate in the elimination round." Though Genevieve controlled her tone, fury laced each word. Her chin lifted.

Taylor couldn't completely hide his surprised smirk. It wasn't often the judges were defied. "Are you conceding then? Because the only way you stay in this competition is through going head-to-head with Alyssa and winning."

Her chin lifted higher as she stabbed a finger in Will's direction. "I refuse to be treated as a liar when this man has sabotaged me. I don't care what your people supposedly found. I know he did it, and I will no longer be a part of this farce of a show."

With her piece said, Genevieve turned around and stalked off the set. Taylor and Adeline seemed as shocked as the rest of them, while Alyssa looked like a weight had been taken from her shoulders. With Genevieve gone, her chances improved significantly.

"That was unexpected." Taylor cleared his throat. "Alyssa, join the rest of the group, please. Due to Genevieve's departure, the rest of you are safe for the time being. Competition is over for the day."

The remaining eight contestants filed silently out of the studio and into the waiting cars.

7

"Could you be a sweetheart and bring me the foil-covered tray from the kitchen?"

The sound of Nicholas's Hispanic accent made Livvy smile. She'd always been a sucker for an accent, and it was a pleasure to listen to him. Not that she was attracted to Nicholas, especially considering he was closer to the age her parents would be. It worked out perfectly. Not only did she get to enjoy listening to him, she also got to have a father figure during the show. She'd had few of them since her dad's death. It would be nice for a change.

"Of course, I'll get it for you. I can't exactly say no to the man cooking for all of us, now can I?"

"You could." He laughed. "But it would not be my fault when all the burgers ended up burnt."

Livvy headed to the kitchen. A swimsuit- and swim-trunk-clad mob met her on their way out to enjoy the pool. Her bathing suit was under her running shorts and tank top. As soon as she finished helping Nicholas, she'd join the rest of them for the much-needed relaxation after an unexpectedly tense day.

"You aren't thinking of sitting this one out, are you?" Will sidled up close enough that his bare chest nearly touched her shoulder, openly looking her up and down in a way he probably thought was complimentary. He was wrong.

"I was really looking forward to doing a few laps with you."

"I'll be there in a bit." She quickly stepped away, conveniently placing the foil-covered tray between them. "I don't think it's fair to leave Nicholas to do everything himself while we enjoy ourselves in the pool."

"Don't take too long. The sides are done and ready to be pulled from the fridge, and I have no doubt Nicholas can man the grill without you for a bit."

Livvy ignored his wink and turned to take the platter to Nicholas, then plunked it down on the prep table beside the grill as Will swaggered off toward the pool.

"You be careful with that one."

"I'm sorry?" Livvy frowned. Maybe she'd used a little more force than necessary, but she hadn't hurt the table or the tray.

Nicholas's dark brown eyes were stormy as he met her gaze, then tilted his head toward Will as the group walked by just out of earshot. "He likes you and doesn't even try to hide it. But, trust me, he's not the type of man you need. Too full of himself to leave room for anyone else."

The breath that escaped her lungs carried a weight she didn't know she felt. "I've been told. I thought it was only for show, but I'm beginning to believe otherwise. I've tried to drop hints that I'm not interested, but he doesn't seem to get it."

"His type doesn't deal in hints. You have to be blunt."

"I'm not sure I can do that. We have to live together for the duration of the taping. I don't want any more drama than we already have. Live in peace with everyone as much as you can and all that."

"Anything else will not work. But I understand your dilemma. Promise me you'll let me know if things get out of hand. I have a daughter about your age, and I know a thing or two about handling overzealous men. You remind me of my Isabel, full of life and kind to a fault. I knew it the moment you went to help Emma. Not everyone would help in those situations."

"You did."

A blush crept up his neck into his cheeks.

Livvy couldn't hide her smile as she threw her arms around his shoulders and kissed his bearded cheek. "Thank you, Nicholas. I feel better about things, knowing you're here to help."

———

EVAN WATCHED Livvy hug Nicholas and kiss his cheek. The display didn't faze him in the least. Nicholas bunked with him and David, and the man was one of the good ones. With a daughter about Livvy's age, it had been natural for him to take note of Livvy's issues with Will. He and Evan shared the worry that it could end up putting her in an uncomfortable position.

Out of the corner of his eye, Evan saw Will standing in the water at the pool's edge and shifted focus to him. Apparently, he'd seen the father-daughter moment between Livvy and Nicholas as well. Only he seemed to read something more into the situation. His jaw was set, and the hand resting on the pool's rim was clenched in a tight fist.

Evan pulled himself from the pool and wrapped a towel around his waist before making his way to the patio. Nicholas and Livvy were in comfortable conversation, oblivious to the waves of animosity emanating from the pool.

"I'm so sorry. Has she been gone long?"

"She died when my Isabel was six years old." Nicholas used the long-handled spatula to transfer a burger from the grill to a waiting platter. "It's been only her and me ever since. She's my world."

Evan hid his surprise. He and Nicholas had talked about family. He knew Nicholas and Isabel were close, but he hadn't realized Nicholas was a widower and single father. What wasn't surprising was Nicholas's choice to confide in Livvy.

In their few conversations, he'd found her genuine and easy to talk to. He hesitated to interrupt but turning around now would seem awkward.

"How's the water, Evan?" Nicholas pointed the spatula toward the pool.

"Perfect. It couldn't be otherwise with temperature controls. But I had to find out, how long before dinner? The burgers smell great, and I'm starving."

"Good." Nicholas chuckled as he pulled another patty from the grill. "They're just about done. Maybe five more minutes. With only Isabel, I tend to forget how young men are always ready to eat."

Livvy placed a hand on his arm. "I'll go get the side dishes so everything will be ready when the burgers are done."

Though she didn't come out and ask, the smile Livvy gave him as she walked past him toward the kitchen gave Evan the impression that she wouldn't mind help. Evan hated leaving her to carry everything out, but he needed the time alone with Nicholas. As soon as she slid the patio door shut behind her, he returned his attention to the man at the grill.

"You need to watch yourself."

Nicholas frowned. "About what?"

"You and Livvy looked pretty close even from over at the pool."

The fire in Nicholas's eyes spoke volumes though his voice remained in control. "That is over the line. Livvy is the same age as my Isabel. How dare you insinuate something like that? Especially since we've talked about it before."

With open hands raised in surrender, Evan shook his head. "Easy, Nicholas. I wasn't trying to say I thought something was happening. I know you're just looking out for Livvy, and I'm sure she appreciates it. But I wasn't the only one who saw her hug you and kiss your cheek. Will looked a tad put out by the display of parental affection. I came to warn you, not accuse you. I think you've just made his ever-growing list of enemies."

"Ah, he's jumping to conclusions, and I just did the same. You deserve better than that. I don't see it changing how I interact with Livvy, but I'll be extra careful to watch my back around Will. Thank you." Nicholas scooped the last burger from the grill, placing it with the others on the tray. He turned off the burners and started gathering his supplies.

"Let me get that for you." Evan lifted the now-full platter. "And I think we'd both better continue watching out for Livvy. She doesn't deserve the inappropriate attention, and she doesn't know how to diffuse it either."

LIVVY TENSED in her chair as Will stood behind her and placed a hand on her shoulder. She turned her head just enough to see him and offer a polite smile. "Yes?"

"I've got to run inside to grab a drink. Care to save me a seat?"

Without asking, Evan dropped into the seat to her left. At the same time, Nicholas took the one to her right. The look Evan gave Will was unapologetic. Livvy bit her lip to keep from laughing at the way they intervened to keep her from an uncomfortable confrontation. Maybe it was a little rude, but Livvy wouldn't waste time feeling bad about it, that was for sure.

Knowing Evan and Nicholas understood and were doing their best to help her, not even Will sitting across from her could dampen her appetite. Lovesick looks turned homicidal depending on whether he was looking at her or one of the men on either side of her. But it didn't matter.

The distance Evan and Nicholas put between her and Will was enough to keep him from *accidentally* brushing her hand or shoulder or anything else. He could look however he wanted. She didn't have to pay it any mind.

"I saw your laps in the pool." Will focused his attention on Evan. "You don't have bad form, but I saw some places for improvement. After dinner, I could show you a few tricks."

Choking on her burger, Livvy took a gulp of water to force it down. Here it came. More machismo from Will. At least Evan had more sense than to give in to the challenge.

"No, man." Evan swiped the air in front of him. "I'm good."

"If you want to settle for mediocrity, I guess I'm not one to argue." A raised brow mocked Evan's refusal. "But let me know when you change your mind. We could even have a little race if you're up to it. I went to championships every year of high school when I was on the summer league team, but don't worry. I wouldn't make you look bad or anything."

Livvy bristled as Will pushed harder. She should probably be embarrassed. If Nicholas and Evan were correct, Will was acting out because he'd not gotten to sit next to her. Since Evan prevented him, Evan was the focus of this attempt at humiliation. Bad move on Will's part. His behavior simply made her mad.

Evan took another bite of his burger and considered Will with a look of boredom as he took his time chewing his food. "Whatever, man." He looked around her to Nicholas. "You do some mighty fine grill work, Nicholas. These are the best burgers I've had in a while."

"Pastry may be my calling, but grilling has always been my hobby."

"It's a hobby you excel at." Livvy smiled at him. "On my night to cook, we'll have to have takeout."

"You don't cook?"

Divulging her secret hadn't been the plan. Her cheeks flamed as it seemed all eyes were on her. Of course, that part could be her imagination. "Not really. Baking is one thing. Cooking is entirely different, and I've never had the inspiration to get better at it."

"If you want to share days, I'm sure we could find enough

inspiration for you." Will's hand stretched across the table to rest on her wrist.

She jerked her hand from under his and into her lap. "I'm sure no one will mind takeout for one night." Scathing remarks flooded her mind. No—be better than that. Be the bigger person. He might be interested in her, but he was only managing to get under her skin.

Could that be his point? Maybe he wasn't into her. It could be an act. Maybe his plan was to throw her off her game just enough to get her eliminated from the competition. And if he was that conniving, was it that much of a stretch to wonder if the judges were wrong? Were Genevieve's accusations correct? Had Will sabotaged her?

"No one will complain about takeout." Evan pushed his empty plate away and stretched, placing one hand along the back of Livvy's seat. "Don't worry about it. You'll find inspiration in other places."

The heat that had filled her cheeks after her admission returned with a vengeance. Confusion swirled her thoughts into an indiscernible mess, and wobbly gelatin replaced her insides. She and Evan weren't an item; they were friends.

Livvy was certain his words were for Will, though he looked only at her. Swallowing, she glanced at Nicholas. He seemed at ease with the situation, though he'd already shown his protective nature where she was concerned. Why wouldn't he feel the same about Evan's gesture? A spark of something she'd never seen before flashed in Will's eyes as he glared at Evan.

The situation was escalating. Where it would end was anyone's guess, but Livvy didn't want to find out. She stood and picked up her plate before reaching for the empty one Evan had pushed away.

"It looks like everyone is finishing up. Why don't I take care of these so you can all go enjoy the pool? I'll come back out and join you when I'm done."

Nicholas stood beside her. "I'll give you a hand. Two will get the job done quicker."

As long as it wasn't Will offering, Livvy was happy to have the help. And maybe Nicholas could shed some light on what was happening at the table. He seemed to have an understanding that went far beyond her limited experience where men were concerned. Her only need was to figure out how to ask without sounding like a complete infant.

"Ah, Livvy, you have got to be careful. Will becomes bolder every time you fail to shut him down completely."

Maybe she really was naïve. "I know. But how am I supposed to do that? And now do I have to worry about Evan, too? He's taunting Will for no good reason."

Nicholas started the dishwasher and leaned against the counter with his arms crossed. "It's not for no reason."

Her frustrated breath momentarily lifted the bangs from her cheek. She brushed them behind her ears. "Other than trying to bait Will, to make him angry—what reason could he have? It's a stupid macho rivalry, and it'll go too far one of these days."

His laugh should have insulted her, but Livvy knew that wasn't his intention.

"You are so much like my Isabel, except in matters of the heart. Tell me, did you grow up with brothers in your house?"

"No. I'm an only child." She frowned. Did it make a difference?

"What about your papa when the boys started giving you attention? How did he react?"

Livvy shrugged. "My parents were killed in an accident when I was young, and then I lived with my grandmother until she died a few years ago. Even if boys had paid me attention, there wouldn't have been anyone there to approve or disapprove."

"I'm sorry, Livvy. I had no idea." He rubbed his chin before dropping his hand to his side. "But what do you mean *if* they paid you attention? You didn't socialize with the other high schoolers?"

"Sure, I did. I was always hanging out with friends in my youth group and school clubs, but just because boys liked me didn't mean they liked me, you know? I was one of the guys. And in college, I was too focused on getting my degree and opening my cupcake truck to socialize. It was pretty much me and my best friend Tabitha at that point. It still is."

The look of disappointment on Nicholas's face confused her.

"I think you're wrong." He paused, weighing his next words carefully. "I've watched you the last few days. You're a vibrant woman with a kind heart. Even a pompous jerk like Will can see it, and he's drawn to it. I think you've known more attention from guys than you realize, and maybe your inexperience kept you from encouraging them to be brave and ask you out."

It was Livvy's turn to laugh.

His brows rose in an unspoken challenge. She stopped. "You're serious."

"Yes, I am. You're starting to see it with Will because he's so blatant in his bids for attention. But you don't see it with Evan."

"Evan and I are just friends."

One shoulder lifted. "For now. And I'm not saying you should discourage him like Will. He's nothing like Will. Evan seems to genuinely like you as a person, and he steps in to keep Will at bay. But given half a chance, I think that boy could easily fall in love with you."

Livvy watched those in the pool from the patio door. She'd noticed Evan stepping between her and Will on various occasions. But he, like Nicholas, was only trying to protect her from unwanted flirtation. That's why he draped his arm around her chair at dinner tonight, to warn off Will. Wasn't it?

Nicholas had to be wrong. Contrary to what he suggested, she'd never gotten any extra attention from guys in her life. And the one time she tried to let a guy know she was interested in him, well, it hadn't worked out in her favor. She didn't get guys' attention, except for what Will was directing her way. And he could keep that to himself.

"I didn't mean to upset you, only to open your eyes to what I see happening. The dishes are done. Why don't you go out to the pool with the others and enjoy the evening?"

"You're not coming?" She looked at him over her shoulder.

"No. No one wants the old man of the group ruining the party. Besides, I could use some peace and quiet. I've not been in a house this noisy since Isabel brought home her girlfriends every weekend in high school."

"It's not true, you know. You'd never ruin the party." She turned and hugged him.

Wrapping his arm around her shoulder, he returned the gesture. "What's this for?"

"Just a thank you for watching out for me. Isabel is lucky to have a father like you. I'm going to the pool. You enjoy your quiet time." She left him standing by the patio door as she made her way to the side of the pool.

As she slipped out of her shorts and T-shirt and placed them in a deck chair, the whistle from the pool made her stomach sink.

"Looking good, Livvy. Come join me, and I'll show you a few strokes."

Did he never quit? Strategically placed cameras watched their every move from the sidelines. Were his antics going to end up in every home in America? What if her customers saw it? What if sweet little Abbie saw it? Would she want Abbie thinking it was okay for men to treat her like that as she got older? Nicholas was right. It was time to stand up for herself.

"Knock it off, Will." Livvy pushed back her shoulders and turned to face him. "I don't find your brand of interest flattering or appealing. If you want a friend, I'm willing. But this has got to stop."

The other occupants of the pool stood in shocked silence.

Will's jaw set before he broke out in a smug smile. "I'm more than happy to be friends, for now. But I guarantee before this show is over, you'll change your tune."

"Leave her alone," Evan spoke from behind Will. "She's trying to let you down easy. Let it go."

"You stay out of this." Will spun to face him. Not even the fact that Evan towered over him gave him pause. "Anyone can see why you're so concerned with Livvy. Don't pretend. We both know, when push comes to shove, which of us is the better man, don't we?"

"Do we?"

"Yeah, we do. You act all cool, but you're a coward. Wouldn't even take up the challenge to race with me. And you think you're man enough to tell me what to do." His eyes strayed to Livvy.

Evan stepped closer. His voice was calm and low. "You want to race? Fine. We'll race. Just don't say I didn't warn you."

The pool emptied, and Evan and Will took their places at the far edge. David was drafted to start the race. Down and back four times would be as close to a 200-meter race as they could manage without properly measuring. Both men stretched, loosening their limbs, then dropped into starting position. David called the start, and there was barely a splash as the swimmers dove into the clear water.

The hamburger Livvy had eaten for dinner churned in her stomach. Nicholas was wrong. This was nothing more than two boys trying to prove who was manliest. But, in his defense, Evan's attempt seemed to stem from his desire to take Will's attention off her. It was misguided, sure, but sweet.

Everyone around the pool cheered for Evan. Livvy felt a little sorry for Will's lack of support until she considered the way he'd treated every last one of them.

After the seventh turn, Livvy moved to the end of the pool, where the winner would be decided. It wouldn't be close, but she wanted to be there anyway. Evan had pulled ahead in the first fifty yards with his smooth strokes and perfect turns; Will never came close. But she had to admit he'd tried hard and hadn't quit. Evan touched the wall and stood up as he waited for his opponent to catch up.

"Good race, Will." He extended his hand. "You're a worthy competitor."

Will ignored the gesture and stalked toward the house without a word to anyone. Nobody else seemed to mind as they jumped back in to enjoy the water.

Livvy frowned at the door closing behind Will. He'd brought it on himself, but losing was not acceptable to someone like him. It had to be a hard lesson to learn on national television. "Do you think I should go talk to him?"

"Definitely not." Evan advised. "He'd probably get the wrong idea. Give him time. He needs taken down a notch or two. Anyway, I doubt he'd do anything except make excuses as to why he lost tonight."

As Evan lifted himself from the pool, Livvy tried not to stare. She'd known he was far from scrawny, but his tanned abs and muscular chest were highlighted by the setting sun. Watching him brush a hand through his long, wet hair did nothing to return Livvy to her senses. On the contrary, every muscle seemed to stand out that much more.

Forcing her eyes to look anywhere but at him, she tried for nonchalant. Maybe he didn't notice. Please, say he didn't notice.

"You're probably right." She hoped her voice didn't sound as breathless as she felt.

Evan toweled off as he walked over to the deck chairs with Livvy following. After he dropped into one, she claimed the one next to his. She couldn't ignore her frustration that he'd even agreed to the spectacle, but he'd gotten Will's attention off her for the duration of the race and hopefully for the rest of the evening. She couldn't find it in herself to be sorry about that.

Whether it was due to Evan's choice to race or her talk with Nicholas, Livvy found herself searching for something to discuss. She and Evan had been at ease with each other from their first meeting, and the awkwardness which currently left her struggling to start a simple conversation felt strange.

"Where'd you learn to swim like that?"

A lopsided grin revealed the deep dimple in the scruff on his cheeks. "Did I forget to mention I went to college on a swimming scholarship? I know my way around a pool as well as I know my way around a kitchen."

Livvy giggled. "Aren't you full of surprises? I don't think Will appreciates it, but maybe it will cause him to think twice before acting so cocky in the future."

"I doubt it."

"You don't like him much. Why?"

"Do you?"

"No." She shook her head. "He's rude and arrogant. Not to mention he's seemed to single me out for some reason."

She couldn't tell if it was a sigh or a disbelieving huff that escaped Evan's lips.

"I told you why, and it's becoming more blatant every day. He's not taking no for an answer where you're concerned."

Curiosity got the better of her. She wanted to know if there was truth in Nicholas's theory. "Is that why you step in? To protect me from his advances?"

He regarded her until she had to look away. Those gorgeous eyes had waffled between gray and green all day. It seemed intense situations tilted the scale in favor of green and looking away was the last thing Livvy wanted to do, but she needed to. Anything else would be too telling. From the corner of her eye, she saw him look back out over the pool.

"Yeah."

How could one small word, not even a word, say so much? Livvy shifted in her seat as Evan looked at her. Traveling down to her toes and back again, his gaze was nothing like the look Will had given her earlier. Nicholas had to be wrong. It was only the beginning of friendship between them.

"What's up with you and the retro look?"

"What do you mean?"

"Your suit is very retro."

Livvy ran her hand across her middle. She loved the modesty

of her red suit with its large white polka dots. The legs weren't cut as high as other suits, and the sweetheart neckline with straps that tied behind her neck was cute without showing too much. It was very much her.

"It's just a suit I saw and liked."

"No. There's more to it. You've got a trendy stripe in your hair, but in competition you wear these vintage-looking aprons and headbands. Your suit screams fifties as well. And I saw your bike out front; not vintage, but it's a throwback in style."

Livvy shrugged. "I like old things, I guess. My mom taught me to bake when I was in grade school. I loved her collection of old aprons from when she was growing up. Whenever we baked anything, she would put Glenn Miller on, and we'd dance around the kitchen having fun while whatever we were making was in the oven."

The sunset ushering in twilight was only half as breathtaking as Evan's smile. "I bet she's proud of you for getting to compete on *Cake That*."

"I don't know." Livvy looked away. "She and my dad died when I was in junior high—car accident. I should have been with them, but I wanted to stay at my grandma's house. Mom loved to bake with me, and those are some of my best memories. She was great at it too. I mean, she could have won this competition, hands down. I can only hope I'm good enough to make her proud."

"I'm sorry. I had no idea."

Emotion clogged her throat. She cleared it and tried to give him a reassuring smile. "It was a long time ago. My mom was an amazing woman. If I knew I was making her proud, well, nothing else would mean as much. But those memories of her are where my love of baking and all things retro started, and as silly as it sounds, they keep Mom close to me."

"No, I get it. I brought the beanie my Gram knit for me, and I feel the same way every time I wear it. I wouldn't be here if it weren't for her, and it's nice to have the connection."

They sat in silence, watching the others in the pool. Livvy wanted to say something, but she had no idea what it should be. She was thankful their ease with each other had returned. But how did one exit such a heavy topic of conversation with grace?

"Glenn Miller, huh?" Evan had been so quiet his voice startled her.

She grinned. "Of course. I am Olivia Rae Miller, after all. Every time she put on one of his songs, my mom would tell me we were only a few steps removed from big band royalty. She claimed Glenn Miller was a distant relative. Apparently, my dad's mom had told her the same thing when she and my dad were dating."

"Wow."

"I don't know if it's true or not."

"Fact or fiction, it's a great story you've got there."

"I suppose it is." Livvy leaned against the back of her chair.

She and Evan continued talking until everyone decided it was time to abandon the pool. Will was nowhere to be found as they came inside, and that suited Livvy perfectly. The last thing she needed was another run-in with him. He could hide in his room to sulk about losing the race all he wanted if it meant a little peace for her.

And it had been a peaceful night, despite the initial drama and the lingering questions Nicholas had planted in her heart. If she could be certain tomorrow's competition would be less disastrous than today's, she could sleep without a care.

8

Camera operators and crew members huddled behind Nicholas's station. Livvy couldn't see what he was doing from her position across the room, but it was interesting enough to draw the attention of the higher-ups angling to make the segment more compelling. She felt sorry for Harper and Evan, though.

While the crew was busy trying to get the best shots of Nicholas, they couldn't help invading the adjacent workspaces. Evan practically had to muscle his way through to the ovens, and Harper had to ask them repeatedly to step away from her counter space.

At least she could work relatively distraction-free on her side of the room. It was beyond her why they couldn't have moved Evan or Harper to Genevieve's vacated spot. She glanced over and was surprised to find both stations next to her empty, though Will's showed signs of activity.

Strange. Where had Will gotten off to? It wasn't like him to leave his station. Oh well, as long as he wasn't bothering her, she really didn't care. Besides, she had to concentrate on her Christmas-inspired creation. Even if it was December, getting in the holiday spirit with palms and pools outside was as difficult as it was necessary to keep her from ending up in the bottom two.

"Smoke!"

Livvy jumped at the single word, unaware of who had said it. She spun toward her oven. Everything looked good there. Each oven on their wall seemed to be in working order. Looking across the room, she saw the problem. Gray plumes billowed from the sides of one of the ovens behind Evan, Nicholas, and Harper. The stinging smell accompanying it penetrated the entire kitchen in seconds.

Crew members set up fans to blow the smoke out of the workspace. Evan jerked open the door and jumped back as a stench-filled cloud tried to envelop him. He waved towels in the air, sending the smoke in the same direction as the fans. Livvy's heart sank. This could be a devastating setback for Evan.

A quick look at the countdown clock confirmed it. There wasn't time to get another cake done for the competition. Evan was headed for the elimination round. It was a depressing thought. She enjoyed her growing friendships with him, Harper, and Nicholas and hated to think about any of them leaving. She refused to consider why the possibility of Evan being eliminated seemed worse than any of the others.

But she couldn't let that distract her now if she wanted to steer clear of the elimination round herself. She wanted to help as she had with Emma, but her creation for this round took precise timing and more intricate decorative work. There was no way she could help Evan and finish her cakes. If her calculations were wrong, she would jump in at the end to help him salvage what she could, but until then, she had to concentrate.

Nicholas crossed over to Evan's station mid-round, but it appeared Evan sent him back without accepting help. He must have realized the competition's time constraints prevented him from redeeming the situation.

Livvy put the final touch on her creation. The countdown clock ticked off the round's remaining seconds, leaving her without enough time to help Evan. She'd finished her best entry in the contest so far, but the various elements had eaten away at her time.

All that was left was facing the judges, and Evan was the first to present.

The large tray he carried to the judging table held only two cupcakes. While they looked perfect, the negative space on the tray shouted his failure to everyone in the room. He set the tray down and stepped back with his head held high. Livvy's respect for Evan as a chef grew as he waited in silence for the judges' remarks. He didn't have to wait long. Adeline immediately touched on the earlier commotion.

"It seems your oven got away from you today, Evan."

His head dipped in a slight nod. "Yes, ma'am."

Taylor plucked a cupcake from the tray. "What exactly happened?"

"I have no idea. The oven was set at the perfect temperature when I put the cupcakes in to bake, but my cake wasn't ready to go in at that time. I didn't touch the controls when I switched them out. However, after I removed the burnt cake and the smoke cleared, I realized the dial had been turned up to over five hundred degrees."

Adeline straightened her shoulders. "Are you claiming sabotage as Genevieve did?"

"No, ma'am. I'm simply stating the facts. I have no idea what happened here today."

Some of the starch fell away from Adeline's posture. Good. His refusal to cast blame seemed to score Evan some goodwill with the judges. They would respect that far more than Genevieve's finger-pointing and blame-casting. Livvy glanced at the other competitors. Will seemed pleased and his disappearance at the time of the disaster weighed on her mind. But was he enjoying the drama because his rival was in trouble or because he'd orchestrated it to begin with?

Evan looked disappointed but not devastated when he

rejoined the group and the next competitor stepped forward. Livvy examined the judges' expressions with each bite they took, but it was pointless. Bland boredom filled their faces. She would hate to go against them in a game of poker. They hid every thought with practiced perfection. Livvy was the final competitor to step forward for judgment; at least she wouldn't have long to wait.

The white decorator sugar dusted over her snowy yule log sparkled under the studio lights as she set her tray on the table. It was the ideal aesthetic to match the marzipan holly leaf and berry twig she'd draped over and alongside the log to add a pop of color. With two holly leaves and berries decorating the matching cupcakes, the effect was everything Livvy had hoped.

Pleased with her effort, Livvy addressed the judges with confidence. "This is my take on the traditional yule log. The sponge inside is vanilla, and the cream in the roll is peppermint. I wanted the naturally stronger peppermint to complement the vanilla, so I added extra vanilla to the cake and the filling."

"And is the filling also in your cupcakes?" Adeline's tone left no doubt that it had better be.

"Yes. I cored the cupcakes and added a dollop of the filling to each one. The marzipan holly decorations are completely edible, and I used sparkling white sugar to recall fresh snow and ice. I hope you enjoy it."

Within minutes of rejoining the group, everyone was called forward for the judges' ruling. Each contestant seemed to understand there would only be one unknown competitor going to the elimination round this time. Evan had not completed his cake. There was no way he would escape the challenge, even if he had impressed the judges with his refusal to whine or place blame.

Adeline's hands came together in front of her in the gesture Livvy was beginning to realize signaled the time of judgment. "With a theme as flavorful as Christmas, we expected to find the comfort of the season in your offerings without sacrificing originality. We were duly impressed."

A wave of relief was almost tangible as it moved throughout the group. Even with the announcement of the bottom two still to come, knowing the judges hadn't been disappointed gave each of them hope that the coming remarks wouldn't be scathing. Before they could relax too much, Adeline continued.

"Of all the entries, two stood out from the rest. Livvy, your new take on the traditional yule log was beautiful. More than a work of art in its design, the flavors evoked a sense of the season. The vanilla and peppermint were balanced with precision. You are safe from the elimination round today."

Livvy didn't even try to stop her broad smile at Adeline's high praise. Other competitors patted her on the back as she passed by them to find a seat in the viewing area. The judges' praise of her yule log, singling it out as one of the best of the day, was more than she'd imagined. She wouldn't forget the sweet feeling of accomplishment any time soon.

"The other stand-out today was a complete surprise." Taylor continued. "Evan, your citrus and spice cupcakes were original and absolutely delicious. We even got a sense of your decorative style with the candied orange segment you included in your frosting. However, we were disappointed knowing we couldn't sample the cake itself."

It could've all been an act for the camera, but Taylor's apologetic look as he paused seemed genuine. "It was an unfortunate turn of events that prevented you from completing the main cake. We're sorry for that, but it's left us no choice. Even with the excellent flavors of your cupcakes, Evan, you will be going to the elimination round today."

"I understand, sir." He nodded, looking resigned but not defeated.

Adeline's hands came together again. "Those joining Livvy in the viewing area today are Nicholas, David, Will, and Harper.

Elliott and Alyssa, one of you will join Evan in the elimination round. The other will watch from the viewing area."

"You have been here before." Taylor looked directly at Alyssa. "And you escaped the elimination round by a twist of fate. You may not be so lucky this time. Your flavors and design were good but not great. The dryness of your cake was improved from last round, but there is still room to perfect it."

"Your efforts these past few days of competition have been enough to keep you safe." Adeline neither smiled nor frowned as she considered Elliott. "But you've failed to stand out. Today, your fruitcake-inspired offering finally helped you do that. It's unfortunate because it didn't make you stand out in a positive way. The flavors were muddled, and the texture wasn't pleasant. It was a brandy-soaked mess. Elliott, you will join Evan in today's elimination. Alyssa, you can join the others in the viewing area."

Elliott seemed nice enough next to Will's over-the-top arrogance, but Livvy still couldn't shake the feeling that he took too much pride in his baking pedigree.

She watched him and Evan work with equal proficiency and confidence as they created their elimination round offerings. Though she shouldn't wish him ill, she hoped they'd say goodbye to him at the end of the head-to-head competition instead of Evan.

Adeline called time as the clock reached zero. "Gentleman, please bring your creations to the judging table."

Stopping short of crossing her fingers, Livvy sucked in a deep breath. Superstition and luck didn't have a place in her outlook on life. God was her source of hope, not rabbits' feet and wishing stars. While she hoped the best for Evan was a win, she could admit she didn't know what would be best for him in the long run. Whether he won or lost, Livvy would simply have to deal with it.

9

"Pass me the salad, please."

Livvy couldn't help grinning as she handed the bowl to Evan, sitting safely beside her. The competition hadn't even been close. Without another oven malfunction to mess him up, Evan executed his dessert flawlessly. Elliott's had been good, but not good enough to send Evan packing.

"That was an interesting turn of events in competition today."

Every muscle in Livvy's body tensed. Why couldn't Will leave well enough alone?

"I don't know what you mean." Evan placed the salad bowl on the table and reached for the garlic bread.

"You mess up and destroy your cake but still manage to impress the judges enough to keep you around. Seems pretty lucky to me."

Evan stopped with the bread halfway to his mouth. "Are you insinuating something?"

"Fine. I think you got to the judges. There's no way you produced such amazing cupcakes that they would overlook your failure to produce an actual cake."

"They didn't. I'm not sure what elimination round you were watching, but I was right there in the thick of it."

"Still. It seems a little unbelievable that you go into the elimination without even finishing the first round and manage to come out on top. Don't you think so, Livvy?"

She couldn't stop her glare as she finished her bite of pasta. Rather than answer immediately, she took a drink of her tea. "No. I don't think so, as a matter of fact. Have you ever watched cooking competition shows like this one? Things like that happen all the time.

"Besides, the first round of competition doesn't have anything to do with judging in the elimination challenge. It's a brand-new competition. And this time Evan out-baked Elliott. It's as simple as that. Now, if everyone will excuse me, I think I'm done with dinner for this evening."

Livvy cleared her plate and glass from the table and took them into the kitchen. It wasn't her night to clean up, but she wouldn't leave more mess than she had to for whoever had the job.

With her things loaded into the dishwasher, she considered her options. Though she didn't want to go to her room, going anywhere Will could show up was out of the question. He managed to get under her skin at every turn. She needed peace and quiet, but leaving the house was against the rules. Contestants weren't supposed to have contact with the outside world unless the producers arranged it.

The hot tub sounded soothing, but it wouldn't be an escape from Will's attention. There was the enormous tub in her room, though. It was deep, and the room was peaceful. She could think, and no one would bother her.

With her destination decided, Livvy took the stairs two at a time and gathered her things while the tub filled. A few drops of lavender oil lightly scented the hot water. She took advantage of the candles in the room and shut off the overhead lights before folding a towel to use as a pillow and sliding into the water.

Steam surrounded her and she breathed deeply, enjoying the release of tension after too many hectic days. The only thing that could make it better was some soft music from her phone. But rules were rules, and the rules of this particular contest plainly stated there were to be no electronics that could connect them to the outside world.

No phone meant the heat, lavender, and candlelight would have to work their magic all on their own. As thoughts of the previous days tried to steal her peace, Livvy knew it was time to pray.

She'd been praying all along. Seeking God in her daily life was natural to her, but she hadn't taken the extra time she usually set aside to tell God all that was on her heart. More than that, Philippians instructed her to seek His answer with thanksgiving and praise, but the busyness of competition and the lack of her daily routine had intruded. It was her fault, and it was time to correct her failure.

Livvy leaned her head back against the makeshift pillow and closed her eyes. She'd always been comfortable making her conversations with God audible, and the possibility of having to explain that to her roommates wasn't going to deter her now. In a quiet voice that fit the atmosphere of the room, she confessed her failure with a repentant heart.

"Lord, I'm so sorry. You deserve more than the limited time I've given You during my time here. I came to You for direction in whether I should enter, and I've thanked You for the opportunity and experiences You've given me during this time. But I've not given You more than in-the-moment prayers since I've been here. You deserve my best, and I feel I've only given my leftovers.

"Please forgive me for letting circumstances steal that time from both of us. Thank you for showing me where I've failed and for forgiving me. Thank you for this opportunity to grow as a person and as a believer. Help me show Your love, grace, and mercy throughout the remainder of this competition. Help me live at peace with each member of this house, as much as it's in my power.

"Give me wisdom in dealing with Will. He tries my patience, but I know he needs to see You in me. No matter what happens, help me remember to give You the praise and glory for all things. Amen."

In the silence following her prayer, the words of some of her favorite worship songs came to mind. Livvy quietly sang each one, meditating on their meanings. When she'd exhausted those, she was content to sit in the silence, letting God fill her heart and mind with His peace and love.

Without a clock in the room, Livvy lost track of time as she spent time resting with God. Her muscles and mind were completely at ease when a knock sounded on the door. She started, and the water around her swirled. When had it turned so cool? She must have been soaking longer than she thought.

"Yes?"

"It's Harper. I just wanted to check on you since you left dinner so quickly. I mean, I don't blame you. Will is a little much to handle. It must be worse for you since he focuses all his attention on you. Anyway, Will, Alyssa, and David are out in the hot tub, but the rest of us didn't really feel like it. We're hanging out in the fireplace room if you want to join us. If not, that's okay, too. I figured I should let you know. But, again, if you don't want to, I understand. No pressure."

Thankfully, Harper couldn't see her through the door. The way she rambled on reminded Livvy of the awkward kid at school who wanted a friend but wasn't quite sure how to make it happen. It was so sweet, Livvy couldn't help smiling. That hint of vulnerability she heard in Harper's voice made Livvy want to reach out and put her at ease.

"I'm glad you did. You go ahead, and I'll join you as soon as I get dried off."

The fluffy towel Livvy wrapped around her was as soft and plush as it looked, and she sighed with contentment. She could put on pajamas. They would be comfortable, but no one else would be in sleepwear. At this point, she didn't need to draw extra attention to herself. Opting for shorts and a T-shirt, she pulled her hair back into a ponytail and headed down to the sitting room. Better to be a little more presentable in mixed company.

EVAN WATCHED Livvy enter the room and immediately look for a place to sit. On either side of the loveseat where Evan sat, Nicholas and Harper perched in plush armchairs. It wasn't planned, but he couldn't deny a bit of satisfaction as Livvy chose to sit beside him. True, it was either that or sit by herself in one of the other chair groupings scattered around the room, but that wasn't the point.

"Where did you run off to this evening?" Nicholas voiced the question Evan had wanted to ask since dinner.

"I needed some space. I'm a people person, but certain people can test that."

"That boy is going to make everyone lose their minds before this is all said and done." Nicholas rolled his eyes. "I wish the producers would do something about him."

Harper curled her legs underneath her. "You and me both."

"They can't." Livvy shook her head. "He's not done anything wrong as a contestant. And they wouldn't anyway. The added drama makes for more compelling television."

Evan angled his body to face her. "So, did you have any epiphanies on how to deal with him while you were enjoying your alone time?"

"As a matter of fact, I did."

"Then spill it, girlfriend." Harper leaned closer. "You can't keep it to yourself when you've found the man's kryptonite."

"It's not like that. It's less about Will and more about me. I need to get back to making my faith a priority again. I've slacked off with my prayer and Bible study during the competition. They won't make Will change, and they won't make me like his antics any more than I do now, but they can help me focus on the positives instead of the negatives. And they can remind me to respond in helpful ways instead of lashing out like I've wanted to do so many times."

Harper's brows drew together. "God? That's what's going to help you deal with Will?"

"Yes, my personal relationship with God affects why and how I do everything in my life. As much as I've wanted to vent my anger at Will, I know that wouldn't honor God or help Will see a difference in the way I live my life. If I'm horrible back to him, why would he ever want to know God?"

As Harper shifted in her seat, Evan wondered if Livvy would try to downplay her faith to make her friend more comfortable. A few awkward seconds of silence assured him she wouldn't backpedal. Good. She had been sincere in sharing her beliefs, and he was glad he'd been present for the discussion.

"It's been a long day." Harper covered a quick yawn with her hand. "I think I'm going to head upstairs now." She didn't wait for anyone to comment before making her escape.

Livvy sighed.

"Don't let it get you down." Nicholas patted her hand on the arm of the loveseat. "Not everyone is ready to accept God for themselves, but Harper now knows the reason for the difference she has seen in you and will continue to see as the contest progresses."

"Maybe I should go after her. Try to explain it better." Livvy looked at the empty doorway through which Harper had fled.

"Be patient. The awkwardness will fade quickly enough. And I'm happy you shared tonight. You've reminded me that even though I can't go to mass and daily prayers at my church during the competition, I can still seek God out every day. Thank you."

Livvy smiled and nodded. "You're welcome."

"In fact, I think I'll go do that now while my room is empty."

Though Evan didn't take his eyes off her throughout the exchange, Livvy only faced him after Nicholas left the room. He hated seeing the hesitancy in her eyes, like she was trying to weigh the chances that he, too, would take offense at her words and leave. He wanted to give her the opportunity to speak first, but when she tucked her bottom lip between her teeth, he knew he had to say something.

"You're a Christian, huh?"

She swallowed before answering. "Yes. Is that a problem?"

"No. I'm impressed, actually."

"Why?"

"I'm pretty new at this faith stuff. I can see I've got a lot to learn."

"We've all got a lot to learn." Livvy raised a shoulder to her ear. "Salvation may come from a moment of acceptance, but it takes a lifetime to learn how to live out our faith in the everyday."

"See?" He pointed at her. "That's what I mean. I've never heard it put like that before. And I never would have thought about sharing like you did tonight."

"Please don't put me on a holy pedestal. I fail as often as I succeed. The secret is being honest with God and coming to Him for forgiveness each time I fall. Tonight, you just happened to be around for one of the times I might have gotten it right."

He smiled. The way she spoke about her faith was so natural. Like everything else about her, it seemed genuine.

"I'm glad I was. I didn't grow up in church. My parents and sisters started when I was busy with college and working to pay for my classes. They were always good, loving, giving people. I didn't see why they needed church too."

"So what happened?"

"They invited me to an Easter sunrise service. I went just to be with them. I came away with Jesus as my savior. But there's so much I don't know. Would you mind me coming to you if I have questions about stuff?"

"I'd be honored. I don't claim to know all the answers, but maybe together we can figure them out."

She paused, watching him. He wasn't sure what she hoped to find, but after a few seconds, she continued.

"In fact, I'll do you one better. There's no telling how long either of us will remain in this competition. Why don't we exchange information, and we can keep talking faith and life and anything else we can think of after we get back to our normal lives?"

"I can't think of anything better, Livvy Miller."

Just replaying the conversation in his mind on the way to his room that night got everything inside him all twisted up. On the one hand, it was great to have someone more experienced to talk to about his new faith. On the other hand, every time he talked to Livvy, he found himself more attracted to her.

Under normal circumstances, that wouldn't be a bad thing, but it could be disastrous with the competition in full swing. He didn't need the conflict between his desire to win and his desire to get to know Livvy better. His thoughts could easily be taken up with her all day, every day, and without sharp focus, he could say goodbye to sending his parents on their anniversary trip. They'd done too much for him and his sisters to be shoved to the side for a girl, no matter how much her eyes sparkled when she laughed. No, he had to win this for his family, even if that meant making sure he and Livvy stayed in the dreaded friend zone.

10

"I'm sorry. Can we just go back to being friends?" Harper whispered.

Livvy paused before going through the doors that would take her into *Cake That*'s kitchen and placed her hand on Harper's arm. "We never stopped being friends."

"Great." Harper's face shone with relief. "I couldn't stand not talking to you last night when you came up to the room. I was just caught off guard. Your faith is your business, and it doesn't have to affect our friendship."

"My thoughts exactly. Now, what do you say we go win today's competition?"

With a nod, Harper practically skipped in behind the rest of the group. Livvy shook her head and followed, minus the skipping part. She was happy to know the awkwardness between them had passed, but that didn't embolden her enough to frolic on national television.

A surprise awaited. A giant map of the world hung on a rolling bulletin board to the left of the judge's table. Livvy looked at her fellow competitors only to find them staring at each other. Furrowed brows, raised shoulders, and shaking heads confirmed they were all equally clueless. What had the producers cooked up for the competition?

Taylor and Adeline entered the room and stood to the right of the table, far from the map.

"Before we can begin today's event, we need each competitor to retrieve the colored dart from their workstation." Taylor motioned to their stations. "We will call you up one at a time to throw your dart from the line marked on the floor. Your task today will be to create a cake and cupcakes that reflect the country you hit. Head to your stations. David, you will throw first."

Everyone hurried to their stations as directed before congregating back in front of the board. Jittery movements from the other competitors confirmed they were as nervous about this turn of events as Livvy. They were bakers. What did they know about throwing darts?

When his name was called, David stepped up to the line. He shifted from foot to foot and glanced over his shoulder at the others.

Cheers of "you can do it" and "you've got this" echoed behind him. And though only the cameras could see their support, several gave David thumbs up and encouraging smiles.

He turned to the map and brought the dart up past his ear. His shoulders raised with a huge intake of breath. No one made a sound as they waited for the first throw.

"Wait!" Taylor's voice shattered the silence.

David started, nearly dropping his dart, and gasped for air. What had the show cooked up to raise the stakes this time?

Taylor approached David and held out something dark. A blindfold. This had to be a joke. Bakers weren't known to be expert marksmen. Wasn't a blindfold overkill? And did they have to nearly give one of their contestants a heart attack?

After slipping the blindfold over his eyes, David once again took aim. The dart flew. It missed the board by at least a foot. An assistant retrieved it from the floor and returned it to him. It was likely that Taylor and Adeline's contracts prevented the producers from putting them directly in harm's way. They weren't going anywhere near the action.

"Throw harder this time. You need an extra foot to foot and a half. You can do it." Nicholas encouraged.

Livvy smiled. He sounded like a dad at his kid's first pee-wee baseball game. If he ever got eliminated, it would be to the detriment of the show, not to mention how much she'd miss him.

With the next throw, David's dart found its mark. Livvy clapped for him along with the others, but her mind was stuck on her previous thought. Nicholas would have to be eliminated for her to win. Of course, she'd known that from the beginning. That's how the show worked.

For every individual who won, there were nine who didn't. Three were already gone. She didn't know them well, so their loss didn't mean much to her. But what about Nicholas? Harper? Evan? She was getting closer to each of them with every day they spent together. She liked them. She respected them. But if she won this competition, their dreams would be left unrealized.

"Livvy, go on." Harper's voice broke through before she finished working through her thoughts. "You're up."

How badly was she about to embarrass herself? Livvy rolled the dart between her fingers. She had zero experience with this game. It had taken David two tries to win the privilege of baking with a German theme. Could she manage to land hers in as few tries and without coming up with something impossible like Antarctica?

She studied the board carefully and positioned herself before slipping the blindfold over her eyes. Picturing the map in her mind, she lifted the dart. Her hand shook, and she inhaled deeply to calm the motion and slow her racing heart. As soon as her arm extended in front of her, she let go. A solid thump convinced her she'd at least made it to the board. The cheers from the other competitors told her she had hit the map, and the dart was stuck fast.

She lifted the mask. Taylor was removing her dart from its place—nowhere near her goal of Canada.

"Congratulations, Livvy. Your dessert will be inspired by Russia."

Russia? Livvy forced a polite smile and nod before moving toward her workspace. At least it wasn't Antarctica, but it still left her mind scrambling for any tidbits she remembered about baking in the influential country.

In high school, she'd attempted a Bake Around the World challenge for fun, and Russia was one of the places she'd researched extensively in preparation. She'd not been assigned Russia at the time, leaving her with little practical experience to pull from for this competition, but maybe she would at least be able to use the information as a starting point for her dessert.

While her thoughts revolved around finding the perfect flavors to represent Russia, Livvy was careful to keep her outward attention focused on supporting the rest of the competitors as they took their turns at the marked starting line marked for their throws. Alyssa and Harper's attempts were worse than David's had been.

Neither could hit the board. Members of the production crew scurried to safety when Alyssa's dart flew wide and missed the board entirely. Livvy felt sorry for her, but she couldn't quite keep her laughter contained at the sight of the trio of frightened people diving away from it as if they were extras in a Hollywood drive-by scene.

After several misses, both ladies were allowed to take the blindfold off. Livvy wondered if it was simply to move things along or if it was also for the safety of the crew members.

Nicholas and Evan redeemed the group with their shots. It seemed both hit the target exactly where they aimed and on the first try. As Evan returned to his spot, Will swaggered up to the line for his turn. Livvy dreaded the return to the house that evening. It was sure to be filled with all everyone else had done incorrectly and how he could help her improve her game. Helping the damsel in distress seemed to be his MO, even if she existed only in his mind.

As he released the dart, she held her breath. It reached the intended target but lacked enough force to sink into the cork. Confident he'd hit the mark, Will ripped the blindfold from his head. Confusion turned to a frown as a crew member retrieved the dart from the floor and returned it for a second shot. He snatched it out of the man's outstretched hand with a glare that seemed to blame the man for his failures. Of course, it couldn't be Will's fault. He never failed.

He slid the blindfold back into place and raised the dart a second time, this time lodging it firmly in its landing place on the map. She couldn't tell exactly where it landed, but Adeline removed it from the board and turned to Will.

"It looks like you will be giving us a cake based on the flavors of France. Contestants, you have four hours to craft cake and cupcake combos that would wow the diplomats of your chosen country. Your time starts now."

Livvy flew into action, making it to the pantry before anyone else. Tossing the usual cake ingredients into her basket, she then grabbed a hive-shaped jar of honey from the shelf. She paused to consider various decorative elements, then snatched up corn syrup and a bottle of vodka. After a quick double-check of her ingredients, she hurried to her workstation. She had a lot to get done and not a lot of time to do it.

The image needed to stay firmly in her mind to complete it to her satisfaction. She pulled paper from a drawer in her station and penciled a rough sketch of her design. With a plan now in place, she went to work on the honey-flavored sponge she would cut and shape. She was baking outside the box again. Hopefully, this time, it would be so well executed the judges wouldn't find fault with her idea.

After sliding her cakes into the oven, Livvy went to work

measuring and mixing the correct amounts of sour cream, powdered sugar, and whipping cream for the filling. But would the texture work with the fondant she planned to drape over the cake? She'd never worked with this type of frosting before, and a national competition wasn't the place she wanted to experiment.

Second-guessing could be her downfall. Of course, it could also mean having a Plan B to fall back on if something in the original design didn't work out. Erring on the side of caution, she mixed together a quick buttercream to serve as the frosting under the fondant.

With her fillings and frostings done, her cupcakes cooling, and her cakes waiting to be cut and formed, Livvy made a marshmallow fondant in shades of green and gold and rolled them out as thin as she could. She'd never been a fan of fondant, but it was a necessity for this project. And so far, it was looking great. She covered the fondant with a damp cloth and moved to the far side of the space to carve her cakes into the image from her sketch.

Livvy wiped the back of her hand across her forehead and glanced at the countdown clock. Finished, with five minutes to spare. For the first time during the day's competition, she allowed her eyes to roam around the room. Finishing touches were being added to everyone's cakes. For once, it seemed competition had progressed smoothly.

"Time is up." Taylor stood behind the table. "Harper, please present your cakes."

As each competitor took their place in front of the judges' table, Livvy was impressed with their creations. She wished she could tell if the judges were equally wowed. How had the producers found two people with such great poker faces? She'd studied them carefully during each judging, and she had yet to find their tells.

"Livvy, please come up to the judges' table."

Was that a slight eyebrow raise she saw on Taylor's face as she set her cake in front of them? She couldn't be sure, but she wouldn't blame him if it were. Livvy stepped back with her head held high. She didn't even need to fidget with her polka-dotted apron or funky headband. She loved her cake, and she was sure they would too.

"Please tell us about your creation." Adeline looked pleasant even if she didn't smile.

With or without smiles from the judges, Livvy couldn't contain her own. "What I have for you today is one of the spires of the Kremlin made from my interpretation of the traditional Russian *Medovik* or Honey Cake recipe.

"Usually made up of many thin layers of sponge alternated with a sour cream filling, I kept the original honey-flavored sponge and sour cream and walnut filling while nixing the many thin layers in favor of thicker sponge. I shaped this into the Kremlin spire and covered it in fondant. The cupcakes are the same cake frosted in green and gold swirled buttercream."

"How did you achieve the shine on the fondant swirls?" Taylor examined the cake, knife poised to slice into it.

"I brushed it with a mixture of corn syrup and vodka."

Adeline nodded her approval to Taylor to commence with the cutting of the cake. "Thank you, Livvy."

Though their faces were still impenetrable masks, Livvy didn't care. She knew she'd done well with this set of cakes. Throughout the remaining cake presentations, her nerves were steady. Even knowing judgment was only seconds away couldn't shake her.

"Most of you did remarkably well during this challenge." Adeline folded her hands on the table. "There was one standout we'd like to acknowledge before announcing the competitors who are safe from elimination."

Livvy's heart raced. Her cake was good. She knew it. Could she secure the best cake two days in a row?

"Nicholas, while you didn't give us a traditional Belgian cake, you paid homage to the country's reputation for chocolate with the most decadent chocolate cake I've ever eaten. Not only was the cake beautiful to look at, it was also moist. Using several types of chocolate, from rich, dark chocolates to the white chocolate mousse filling, created a beautiful marriage of flavor. You were the standout today, and you may take your place in the viewing area."

Disappointment stole some of Livvy's pleasure, but she couldn't begrudge Nicholas his win. He deserved to be honored for his cakes. They had been beautiful, and Livvy could almost taste the rich flavors he'd used together. But since the judges were the only ones who got to try the cakes, she'd have to content herself with her imagination.

"As Adeline said, most of you did well today, and it was a hard decision for us." Taylor waved his upturned palm in front of the group. "Will, Evan, and Livvy, please join Nicholas in the viewing area. You are safe for now. Alyssa, Harper, and David, please step forward."

Livvy took her place and prepared to watch two of the three battle it out for the opportunity to bake again.

11

"There's only one question left after today's elimination." Harper skipped up beside Livvy on the walk leading to their temporary home.

"What's that?"

She placed a hand on Livvy's forearm. Livvy turned to face her, eyebrows raised in question.

Harper took a huge breath, and Livvy tried not to react to the melodrama. "Do we stay in the same room we've been in, or does one of us claim the empty one since Alyssa was eliminated? I mean, I've totally enjoyed sharing with you. It's kind of like a sleepover every night, if I had a best friend who was extremely wealthy. But I can see the advantages to having our own space. And it does seem like a waste. Don't you think?"

It seemed cruel to consider a takeover of Alyssa's old room. She hadn't gotten to know her well, but Livvy didn't have anything against the woman, either. Of course, Harper had a point. After botching her elimination round by putting too much artificial raspberry flavoring in her dessert, Alyssa didn't need it anymore. David secured the win, and Alyssa moved out of the house.

The idea of having one of the magnificent rooms to herself

sounded luxurious. Uninterrupted showers and baths, no one snoring in the bed next to hers, and a space where no one else could follow if she wanted to be alone—these were all definite perks to consider. Plus, it wasn't like they wouldn't see each other. She and Harper could still chat any time they wanted.

"You're right." Livvy looped her arm through Harper's and headed for the door. "It would be a shame to waste this opportunity. But I call dibs on staying where I am. You can take Alyssa's room."

"No problem." Harper's laugh made her smile. "Have you seen the view from that room?"

Harper was still moving her things into the new space when the rest of the group finished cleaning up supper and chose chairs around the fireplace. Plans to keep a safe distance from Will evaporated when David excused himself from the sofa. Almost before he vacated the spot, Will claimed it.

Great. She wasn't prepared to walk the fine line of shutting him down without hurting his feelings. Maybe it wouldn't matter. She pressed herself as close to the end of the cushions as possible.

"I hear you and Harper have split up." Will inched away from the end where he sat.

"We weren't exactly a couple, but yeah, she decided to take Alyssa's old room." She fought the urge to roll her eyes. "It will give us both an extra bit of privacy."

His eyes glinted. "Aren't you girls lucky? We guys are still double occupancy. No privacy there. Of course, maybe your privacy could end up being lucky for one of us, too."

Livvy couldn't stop her mouth from falling open. He was not implying what she thought, was he? Her cheeks warmed as temper churned in her chest. She stood and moved away from the couch. One. Two. Three. Forget it. She should cool off first, but she wouldn't make it to five without answering.

"Surely you aren't suggesting what I think you are?"

One eye closed in a quick wink as he stood and moved closer.

Either she was more in control than she felt, or the man was completely clueless.

"I'm only saying there are times when a private room might be a nice perk, especially when there's a woman like you to share it with."

The shock of her palm connecting with his cheek was just the beginning of her anger. "Don't you ever speak like that to me again. I've been nice. I've been patient. I've never encouraged your attention, and I want it to stop now. Are we understood?"

A handprint reddened his cheek, but Livvy refused to cringe. She'd never slapped anyone, never even dreamed there could be a situation where she would. But she had. She shoved the twinge of guilt to the back of her mind to sort through later.

"No, you don't understand." Will's eyes hardened. "I took pity on you and gave you my attention. No idea why. You're only mediocre as a baker, and I bet you're even less of a woman. Being more tolerable than the other women in this place doesn't make you special."

Livvy gulped. When had the air been sucked from the room? She flinched as he took a step toward her, but Nicholas put himself between them.

"Leave her, Will. You've done enough."

"*I've* done enough?" Will jabbed a finger at the shorter man's chest. "I'm not the one slapping people."

"Your words were more than a slap." His head raised in challenge. "Now, I'm asking you nicely to leave her alone."

Evan moved beside Nicholas, folded his arms across his chest, but said nothing.

Will looked at the two men. "You're not always going to be here to butt into things that aren't your business. But whatever." He shifted his attention to Livvy. "You're not worth it."

Without another word, he turned and stalked from the room. As his steps faded from hearing, the cords wrapped around Livvy's lungs fell away. She dropped back onto the sofa, gasping for breath. The fury was gone, but the sting of his words remained.

It didn't matter. His insults meant nothing. It was his bruised ego hurling them at her so carelessly. Salty tears continued to burn her eyes even as her thoughts played on a loop, and she tried to hold them at bay. She closed her eyes against them, but the dam did nothing to staunch the flow. Covering her face with her hands, she gave up the fight.

Livvy barely registered the shift of the cushions as someone sat beside her. The weight of his arm settled over her shoulders, and she let herself be pulled against his side. Tilting her head, she looked into age-wizened brown eyes radiating concern for her well-being.

"I shouldn't have slapped him. Why did I slap him?"

Nicholas's shoulder shrugged behind her head. "Will's been out of line before, but this went far past the line. He needed a wake-up call."

A sigh escaped before she could stop it. "I'm not sure he didn't sleep through the alarm. He didn't seem sorry to me, just angry."

"Anger hides many things in a man. Embarrassment, guilt, sadness. In this case, I'd say it's trying to protect his big ego. You put him in his place, publicly. He'll act out."

"But he won't just act out toward me." Livvy grasped the hand resting on her shoulder. "Nicholas, you stood up for me. You'll be in his line of fire. Evan, too."

Livvy turned from Nicholas as Evan moved to kneel in front of her on the other side and his hand covered hers on the sofa cushion. Did he feel the jolt that his touch sent up her arm? She swallowed, and his head dipped lower as if he wanted her attention. Didn't he realize he had it the second he moved toward her? She raised her gaze to his.

"Nicholas can handle Will. We're worried about you."

"I appreciate the concern." She offered a weak grin before turning it on Nicholas and then back to Evan. "But I don't want you in the middle of it any more than you already have been."

Evan opened his mouth to argue. Livvy held up a hand to stop him.

"You don't know how much it means to me that you've been there for me. But those times, you served as a distraction. This time it was blatant interference. I don't think he's going to forgive that, and I don't want either of you to suffer for it. I know I got upset at his insults, but I'm stronger than that. I promise I am. I can handle Will."

"And if he escalates even further?" Evan's hazel eyes darkened to a deep green.

Did emotion change eye color? Was that a thing? And if it did, what emotion was coloring them now? Jealousy, anger, or concern? But Evan had asked a question. He was waiting for an answer. What was it about? Will. Escalating.

"As long as it's words, I can ignore it or shut it down. If it gets ugly, I'll have no choice but to take it to the producers. I don't want it to come to that, but I don't think speaking with them now would do any good. Drama equals ratings."

Evan pulled the cap from his head and ran a hand through his hair. Despite the seriousness of the situation, Livvy had to fight a giggle. He looked like an adorable little boy with bedhead. But a storm was brewing in his eyes and was evident in the set of his jaw. She knew better than to laugh.

"That's not right."

"No." Nicholas shook his head. "But it's the truth. Shows need ratings, and drama will get people talking. As long as her safety isn't a concern, I think Livvy's wise to keep handling things as she is, and if she needs us, we'll be there for her. And now, I think I'll go up to our room." He planted a fatherly kiss to the side of her head and stood. "It's late for an old guy like me."

"Thank you, Nicholas. Isabel is one lucky girl to have a father like you."

Though he smiled when he looked down at her, it was

wistful. How hard it must be for him and Isabel to be apart. They appeared to be a tight-knit family, something she'd missed out on during her teen years. However long she and Nicholas were both in the competition, she would enjoy having a surrogate father around. Maybe she could even help ease his separation from Isabel.

Nicholas turned to Evan. "I'll see you in our room in a bit?"

Evan nodded from the chair he'd reoccupied. The look that passed between them before Nicholas left the room meant something, Livvy was positive. It felt like Nicholas warning Evan. But Nicholas didn't have a problem with Evan, did he? She waited until she could no longer hear Nicholas's footsteps on the stairs.

"What was that look for?"

"What look?"

"Seriously?" Livvy rolled her eyes. "Don't play dumb with me. Is he mad at you or something?"

One brow lowered as the other rose. "No. Why would you think so?"

This time she rolled her head from one shoulder to the other, as if the simple action could release the tension and frustration of her day, before focusing back on Evan. "I think so because of the look he gave you right before he left. Now, what was it about? Is he worried about leaving me alone with you?"

A grin raised the right side of his lips. "Nicholas has left us alone several times, and it's not bothered him before. Why do you suddenly think he feels the need to warn me away?"

"I don't know. I'm an only child raised by my elderly grandmother. I'm not fluent in the silent communications of men. So, tell me what that was about, please."

The pressure of his hand resting on her shoulder eased her irritated nerves. Earlier signs of amusement had fallen from his features. The indignation that had turned his eyes dark only minutes before had also melted away, leaving concern in their now gray-green depths.

"I'm sorry. I didn't mean to make you feel like I was having a joke at your expense. Nicholas was warning me, but not to stay away from you. He's concerned about Will. He doesn't want you in a situation where you might have to deal with him alone. So, he was asking me to stay with you until you were ready to go to your room."

Her eyes strayed to the stairway just on the other side of the room's doorway. "Nicholas looks out for me like I'm a daughter."

"He does. Are you okay with that?"

"It's more than okay. I haven't had that since before I was a teenager. It's kind of nice. Though I wish there weren't anything for him to be protective about." Her smile at Nicholas's behavior turned into a frown as another thought brought confusion and the slight sting of disappointment. She fidgeted with her hair before getting up the nerve to face Evan again. "Nicholas protects me like a father, and now that he's not here, he wants you to watch out for me?"

"Yes."

"So, he wants you to watch over me like you would a little sister?" The disappointment she'd felt at the thought was currently making her nauseous. A little sister was the last thing she wanted Evan to see when he looked at her, though all his attention could have been precisely that. She was surprised to realize how strongly she wished it wasn't true, but who was she to judge men's interest?

On more than one occasion, Nicholas had pointed out she was naïve in these situations. Besides, should she even want more with Evan? How could she go through life making every opportunity for her dreams to come true, only to now jeopardize her chances of winning the competition with thoughts of romance?

She glanced at Evan and away again before she could make full eye contact. What little she did see pulled her gaze back immediately. "Are you laughing at me?"

"It's got to seem that way, but no." Evan shook his head even as a chuckle seemed to contradict the movement. "I'm just surprised, is all."

"Surprised at what?"

"That after all our conversations and the time we've spent together, you would think I look at you like a sister."

She momentarily clamped a hand over her open mouth. "I didn't mean to insinuate we were close enough for you to think of me as family. I'm so sorry if I upset you!"

This time his laugh was full. "You're missing my point. Livvy, I can't think of you as a sister, but it's not because I don't care."

"Then ..."

"It's because every time I look at you, every time you smile or laugh, I have to fight the urge to kiss you. And that is definitely not the way I feel about my sisters."

Nervous energy pulsed through her. Evan wanted to kiss her. She'd never even dated a guy before, and now one with eyes she could drown in and dimples framing his beautiful, carefree smile wanted to kiss her. Her? The one who'd always been one of the guys? She searched his eyes for signs that he was joking but found an intensity she wasn't sure how to handle.

She licked her suddenly dry lips, drawing his eyes to the movement. He leaned toward her, and her body eased forward in instinctual response. For twenty-four years, she had thought about what her first kiss would be like, but now all ability to think fled.

His fingers wove through her hair as his hand cupped the back of her head and drew her the rest of the way to him. She felt a whisper of breath brush over her skin right before his lips met hers with softness she'd not expected. The warmth of his touch spread from her lips through her entire body. She'd imagined a million different scenarios for her first kiss, but she'd never dreamed up something as sweet or wonderful as this.

Without deepening the kiss, Evan pulled away from her. Livvy could only guess at what he saw as he watched her with mere inches separating them. She fought the urge to look away. What did one do or say after a kiss like that?

"I may be an only child, but I'm certain I wouldn't kiss a brother like that."

Evan's head fell back as he laughed. His smile remained as he brushed the back of his fingers down her cheek. A look she didn't recognize dimmed the light in his eyes, and his smile faded. "No. That was definitely not the way someone kisses a sibling. But it's getting late, and we've got another big day tomorrow. Why don't we head up to our rooms?"

Livvy let Evan lead her from the room. Thankfully, he was in front of her as he took her hand and led her up the stairs. His hand was warm around hers, but that look in his eyes—was he disappointed? Did he regret their kiss?

A simple "good night" was all they said before separating to find their rooms.

Half-wishing she and Harper hadn't split up, Livvy climbed into bed and snuggled deep into the covers. Would the nervous energy she felt dissipate if she was able to talk about the kiss? Squealing like a schoolgirl would bring Harper and everyone else running, wouldn't it? Livvy ran her fingers over her lips as she relived his touch. Her first kiss. Others would probably laugh at that. Twenty-four years old before being kissed for the first time.

Let them laugh. She was old enough to understand kisses weren't like stickers in a kindergarten class to be handed out to everyone who wanted one. They were supposed to mean something.

But what did this one mean? Her heart felt heavy inside her chest. Livvy had a feeling Evan was as surprised by it as she was. She'd thought about it, and now she was sure he had, too. But thinking and doing were two different things. Maybe that's why he'd felt the need to retreat to their rooms. Maybe he needed to find out a way to close the door they'd opened.

Between the instant replay going on in her mind and the questions it left about where they would go from here, Livvy wondered if she was in for a sleepless night. She reached out to switch off the bedside light and turn her mind to prayer. It was the only thing she knew could calm her fractured thoughts. Maybe it would be enough to bring her peace.

DESPITE HIS ANNOUNCEMENT that he needed sleep, Nicholas was lounging on his bed reading when Evan entered their room. Without any other occupants, he knew they could speak freely, but he wasn't sure if there was anything to say or if it would help if he did.

"That's an interesting look. Is there an equally enthralling story to go with it?"

He shrugged. "I don't know that I'd jump straight to enthralling. Interesting? Sure. Confusing? Definitely. Enthralling? I suppose it depends on your definition."

"Do you want to talk about this interesting and confusing situation?"

Did he? Nicholas and Livvy were close. Of course, he was close to Nicholas, too. But would it strain their friendship? He would be living with the man until one of them was eliminated, and Nicholas was also the only one he could talk to freely.

He sucked in a deep breath. Might as well plunge into the deep end. "I kissed Livvy."

One eyebrow raised. Was that a sign of disapproval? Disappointment?

"Well, I mean, she kissed me back and everything. It may have caught her by surprise, but I'll be honest, it did me too."

"Hmm."

"Why aren't you saying anything?" Evan pulled his hat off and tossed it on the nightstand, then ran his fingers through his shaggy hair. "Do you think it was a mistake?"

"The question is, do you think it was a mistake?"

"No." He dropped onto his bed. "Maybe. I don't know, Nicholas. I like her. She's quirky and friendly. And the way she patiently puts up with Will, not wanting to hurt him but still trying to protect herself? I think that proves she's got a caring heart. And her smile, well, you can't help smiling back. She's beautiful."

Nicholas sat up and swung his legs over the side of the bed to face Evan. "You're attracted to her. That much is evident. But that wasn't my question. Was it a mistake?"

"I just don't know." Evan hesitated. "I'm not here for a girl, Nicholas. I'm here to win this competition. I need to win so I can give something back to my parents. They've always sacrificed for my sisters and me."

"What does that have to do with Livvy?"

"I can't get distracted." He looked the older man in the eyes. "If I lose focus, I'll never be able to win. Everyone in this competition deserves their place in it. There aren't any throwaway competitors. Even if there were, the others would prove a challenge."

Frustrated, he stood and paced the aisle between their beds. When Nicholas remained silent, he plopped back onto the bed and continued to share his tumultuous thoughts.

"Besides, one or the other of us has to be eliminated. We're still rivals, and I'm pretty sure girls don't take kindly to that kind of thing. The kiss shouldn't have happened. Now I have to figure out a way to undo it."

A slow shake of Nicholas's head told Evan as much as his words. "In my experience, that is not possible. You may be able to salvage your friendship, but it won't be the same. Livvy likes you, I can tell. She's sweet and smart, but she may not be equipped to understand why you're pushing her away after kissing her. You will hurt her. She doesn't deserve to be hurt, especially not by a trusted friend."

Evan squirmed under Nicholas's direct gaze. The warning was clear inside his admonition. He saw Livvy as a daughter. It only made sense that Nicholas wouldn't want her hurt. Well, neither did he.

Older didn't have to mean wiser. Did it? Nicholas was mistaken. He had to be. Was Livvy a bit naïve where men were concerned? Yes. He'd seen that clearly in her dealings with Will. But she was a beautiful, charming woman. He was sure she'd navigated the rough seas of relationships enough in the past to help her deal with this tiny blip on the radar. It was a simple kiss.

He shoved down the niggling doubt trying to creep through his insides, and looked at Nicholas with what he hoped was calm assurance. "It might sting a little, but Livvy will be fine. Once I explain things, I know she'll understand. For now, let's just get some sleep. Who knows what the show has cooked up for us tomorrow."

12

Livvy rubbed a hand up and down her arm and tried not to glare at Taylor and Adeline standing across from the group, fully awake and clothed in something other than pajamas. At least she could be thankful that she hadn't slept in anything skimpy.

As it was, when one of the show's crew knocked on her door before her alarm had gone off and told her contestants were to meet on the front porch, she'd been able to jump out of bed in long pink plaid pajama bottoms and a modest matching tank top. Harper hadn't fared as well, wearing a flimsy, spaghetti-strapped nightgown that barely hung to her knees.

True, by society's standards it was modest, but Harper's hands hanging down at her sides kept grasping the material and pulling it down as if to make the hem stretch farther down her leg. Livvy wasn't the only one to notice her discomfort. Nicholas removed his lightweight robe and wrapped it around Harper's shoulders, leaving him in a T-shirt and cotton sleep pants. Harper smiled up at him and stopped fidgeting.

Would it have been so difficult to let them get dressed before this early morning meeting? What was so important that the producers had to parade them in front of thousands of viewers before they'd even had a chance to make themselves presentable? Whatever it was, it was most assuredly not as important as they believed it to be.

With everyone in place, the director called them to action, and filming for the day began.

"I'm sorry to wake you all so early, but today's event requires more time than usual." Adeline smiled insincerely. "You'll thank us later for the early start."

"Without a doubt." Taylor continued the scripted dialogue. "Today is a paired event. You and your partner will make your way to the local farmer's market using your own vehicles or one of our show's cars. Once there, you will choose ingredients from the available produce to use in your cake and cupcakes."

Adeline edged forward, drawing their eyes back to her. "Because today's competition requires an extra step, there's a twist in our timing. You have thirty minutes to prepare to leave. After that, you have five hours to get to the market, back to the studio, and complete your cakes for the day.

"Keep in mind, the more time you spend at the market, the less time you'll have to bake. The lowest-scoring team will go to the elimination round. Taylor, please let them know their partners for the day."

"David and Harper. Nicholas and Will."

"No!" Will's voice interrupted the list of partners. "I can't be partnered with Nicholas."

"Why wouldn't you be comfortable with the pairing?" Adeline's head tilted to one side.

"Last night, he threatened me." Will glared at Nicholas. "While I hold no ill feelings toward him, I cannot agree to the pairing. You've got to allow us to switch. I'll even take Harper, and we know she's nowhere near my level of baking expertise."

Harper's eyes grew large. "Hey! What did I ever do to you?"

"Don't pretend." Will barely flicked a glance in her direction. "You know being paired with me could only help your chances in the competition."

"That's enough." Taylor cleared his throat. "This is highly unusual. Nicholas, do you have anything to say about Will's accusation?"

"It's no secret Will is less than friendly toward his competition. Last night, his behavior reached new lows." Nicholas raised his chin. "We had words. Contrary to his assertions, there were no threats. However, if the judges were to see fit to a new pairing, I would not be opposed to that."

Will's jaw tensed. Likely he wanted to press his point but had enough sense to know further argument would not work in his favor. His eyes never wavered from the judges.

One of the producers joined Adeline and Taylor. The contestants waited while the three held a private conference on the lawn in front of them and shot looks in their direction. Heads nodded. The producer went back to his place behind the cameras. Adeline and Taylor resumed their positions.

"Though we feel your explanations have only scratched the surface of last night's issues, we do not have time to deal with them now." Adeline's tone was clipped as she passed down the judgment. "You are not children. You should begin to consider how you can act more like the adults you are in the future. In light of these matters, we will allow a repairing. Nicholas and David are now partners, as are Will and Harper. Livvy and Evan make the third pairing."

Taylor pretended to look at his watch. "You have thirty minutes to prepare to leave. Time starts now."

Without a word, the contestants scrambled to get back into the house and up the stairs. Livvy hurried through the fastest shower she'd ever taken before dressing in the outfit she'd laid out the night before. Without time to do her hair properly, she brushed through it and pulled it back into a low ponytail before sliding on one of her trademark headbands. A quick trip to the closet, and she was out the door.

When the last of the group had returned to the front porch,

the judges handed out the address of the farmer's market. Everyone scattered to waiting vehicles.

Livvy thrust a helmet toward Evan. "Here."

He hesitated. "Why do I need a helmet?"

"I know it's not the law, but I have to insist. Anyone getting on the bike with me has to wear a helmet."

"We're taking your bike?"

"If you're willing. The directions to the farmer's market are pretty straightforward, but Los Angeles traffic is horrible. Taking the bike gives us an advantage. When traffic is at a near stop, I can still find a way through."

"Well, then, lead the way." He slid off the hat his Gram had made, carefully folding and tucking it away, and replaced it with the helmet. He grinned at her, and they headed out.

Focus, Livvy. Focus. She couldn't afford to make a mistake and turn down the wrong road because the man who'd kissed her last night now sat pressed against her back with his well-toned arms loosely hugging her waist. They would not lose their advantage because she couldn't control her hormonal thoughts. She would, however, need to send the producers a gift basket for picking the perfect partner for her.

CONTENT TO LET her lead the way, Evan followed Livvy through the throng at the farmer's market. He had to get a grip on his wayward thoughts. The firm declaration he'd made to Nicholas less than twenty-four hours ago had wilted the moment he'd straddled the motorcycle and placed his hands around the curve of Livvy's waist. His mind still said the kiss shouldn't have happened, but it was reduced to a whisper by the desire to repeat his mistake.

As she grasped his hand, pulling him toward a booth across the aisle from the stand where they'd just purchased an assortment of citrus fruits, his resistance became a pitiful whimper.

"Earth to Evan. Are you even listening to me?" Livvy's amused voice intruded on his wayward thoughts bringing him back to the task at hand.

"I'm sorry. What did you say?"

Livvy rolled her eyes. If not for the grin on her face, Evan might have thought he'd irritated her. As it was, she seemed more amused than anything. If they lost precious time due to his mind wandering, she might lose her good humor. He needed to keep his focus.

"I asked what you thought of this pairing."

"What pairing?"

Only when she lifted both hands to shoulder height and shook them did he notice she had fruit in both. Orange and plum? Could be a winner.

"I like the combo, but what are you thinking?"

Livvy's eyes lit up like the sky on the fourth of July. "As soon as I saw what the market had to offer, it just came to me."

As Livvy laid out her plan, Evan was struck by her creativity. Within just a few minutes of their arrival, she'd already narrowed down their flavor pairing and come up with a basic design concept. She'd done the heavy lifting so far, but Evan determined to pick up the slack for the remaining time.

Lifting the shopping basket from her arm, Evan nodded towards the booths containing the desired fruits. "It sounds great. I'll grab the plums and oranges. You scout out the other booths and see if there's anything else we need to execute your plan perfectly. Meet you at the entrance in ten minutes?"

With a nod and an excited smile that elicited one of his own, Livvy took off in the direction of the booths selling fresh herbs. Evan turned back to the fruit stand to complete the task of choosing the ripest, sweetest fruits for their cakes.

Meeting him at the assigned spot in less than the ten minutes allowed, Livvy took the bag of fruit from his hand. "I'll put these in the saddle bags, and we'll be back to the studio in no time. Ready?"

"Yes, ma'am."

LIVVY AND EVAN pulled into the studio before anyone else. Will and Harper had only just arrived at the farmer's market when they were on their way out. Taking the bike had certainly paid off. It was anyone's guess where Nicholas and David were, but they couldn't think about that now.

Using her motorcycle had secured them a sizable lead, and they weren't going to waste it. She flipped open the saddle bag and removed the produce they'd purchased as Evan held out the loaner helmet.

"Come on." She traded him the bag for it. "Let's get this cake started. Thanks to my ingenious plan, we've got a full three and a half hours to complete our cakes. Lead the way—your workstation or mine?"

Livvy let her mind wander as she cut up plums and dropped them into a saucepan with the other ingredients needed to reduce the fruit to a thick, sweet filling. Evan hadn't said or done anything specific, but the whole morning felt a little off.

One minute Evan was sending waves of warmth through her with his tight hold around her waist. The next, he watched her with a guarded gaze as she picked up the produce for their cake. Then, just when she was convinced something was wrong, he smiled and relaxed like he didn't have a care in the world.

Now they worked and moved as a team in the kitchen, but there was an undercurrent of tension. At least, she thought there was. Then again, she couldn't point to specifics. Could she simply be imagining it?

She gasped as she looked into the pan. She dropped the spatula into the rapidly boiling plum reduction and reached for the burner's knob. How long had it been boiling like that? She had no idea. A quick twist to the right, and she breathed a desperate prayer that she had caught it in time to prevent the filling from scorching.

That was precisely why she hadn't wanted to mix attraction into the competition. It threw her off her game. Hopefully, for both their sakes, it wasn't going to create an inescapable disaster.

By the time Will and Harper ran into the studio nearly forty-five minutes after them, Evan and Livvy had completed their surprisingly unburned filling and the almond cake batter was almost finished baking. While Evan candied slices of plum and delicate spirals of orange peel, Livvy went to work on a ginger buttercream frosting.

Their cake was fully cooled and lacking only finishing touches to the frosting before David and Nicholas sprinted into the studio. Her eyes shot to the countdown clock. They only had an hour left. They didn't waste time before heading to the adjacent workstation to begin their creation. What had kept them out so long? They knew the time clock was their biggest hurdle in creating presentable cakes for the judges.

As she turned back to their cake, Livvy noticed Will across from them. He had paused in his own preparations long enough to smirk as the tardy team raced into position. His pleasure sparked her anger. Livvy turned back to her cake only to realize the dollop of frosting was no longer on her spatula. With her attention averted from her work, it had dropped to the counter. She huffed and wiped away the wasted mess before scooping more from the bowl.

"Don't let him do that to you." Evan's whisper calmed her. "Nicholas is good. He'll be okay. In fact, why don't you head over to their station and see if you can help? We're down to the final decorations, and I can handle that."

"Are you sure?"

He nodded.

"Thank you." She brushed his hand with her own and smiled when what she most wanted to do was kiss him.

How had she ended up getting the attention of such a sweet guy? He wanted to win as much as she did, but he didn't let it keep him from helping a friend. Whatever was bothering him, they'd sort through it and make this work. They were intelligent adults. There had to be a way to work out a relationship and keep her head in the competition.

At the neighboring station, Livvy offered her help. Nicholas pulled her into a hug before putting her to work. They were still working at a frantic pace when Evan put the final orange spiral on their cake and joined Livvy at Nicholas's station.

Even with the extra help, time ran short. Long before Nicholas's team had their cake perfected, the clock flashed a series of zeroes across its screen. Taylor stood behind the judges' table.

"Time."

Livvy glanced at Nicholas. He placed the decoration he held on the workstation. Even rushed for time, he would not test the rules by dropping one last element into place. He and David were both calm, but she could see the resignation in their eyes. This wouldn't go well. She joined Evan back at their station.

"Nicholas and David, please come forward." Adeline clasped her hands in front of her and broke the tense silence in the room.

As David and the man who'd been her champion since the beginning of the show trudged toward judgment, Livvy's heart hurt. Their cake was done, but it was simple and without adornment. Their cupcakes fared no better. They set the unimpressive offering on the table and took a step back into place.

Taylor eyed the cake before looking to them. "David, Nicholas, what happened here? You've given us a cake, but the frosting seems to be sliding off in spots like it's melting."

"We were running short on time." David clasped his hands behind his back. "The cakes couldn't cool properly before time forced us to apply the frosting. I'm surprised it has held up this well."

"You would have done well to take less time at the farmer's market and spend more time on your baking." Adeline steepled her index fingers without unlacing the rest of them.

"Yes, ma'am." Nicholas cleared his throat. "That would have been ideal. But shortly after leaving the house, our car had a flat tire. There was no spare, and we had to wait while Daniel brought one to us. Much of that precious time was spent changing the tire before we even made it to the market."

Taylor looked beyond the stage to the crew edging the filmed area. "Dan, is that how it happened?"

"We're not sure how it happened." Daniel stepped into the staging area where the cameras would see him. "But the tire must have picked up a nail somewhere. And yes, there was no spare. I got a new tire to them as quickly as possible." He tried to keep his expression matter-of-fact, but Livvy noticed tightness in his jaw. And while he stayed respectful, she heard a slight edge in his voice. He'd already expressed his dislike of nicknames. Why couldn't the others seem to remember that as Nicholas had?

Before Daniel could move back into the off-camera edges of the room, Livvy heard a chuckle. She turned from Daniel just in time to see Will cover his mouth as if he'd coughed. The nerve of that guy.

First, he refused to partner with Nicholas, and now he was enjoying the unfortunate events that put the other team in front of the judges with a melting cake. Why couldn't Will have been part of that team?

Wait. He should have been part of it. How did he end up lucky enough to avoid the problem while the man he disliked was stuck with a flat tire? Will seemed to be on the outer edge every time disaster struck but far enough away to keep from getting burned by it.

The judges finished their tasting of Nicholas and David's

cakes and moved on to Will and Harper. Livvy's mind ran through all the events of the previous days. Only one didn't have some kind of calamity, though that one had its own stress since few of the competitors had an aptitude for darts. Emma's cake on the floor, salt in place of sugar, and now a flat tire?

Either there were an unusual number of accidents happening this season, or something else was going on.

"Ready?" Evan nudged her.

Livvy cleared her racing thoughts. It was time to present their cakes. She nodded and waited for him to pick up the serving tray. "Let's go."

After the final cakes were presented, the three pairs stood side by side to hear who was safe and who would have to fight their partner for the privilege of staying in the competition. Before the judges spoke a word, Livvy knew Nicholas and David would be in the elimination round.

Melting frosting drew all attention away from the unfinished presentation, but it wasn't the least bit helpful. She doubted the judges would find even the smallest element to compliment, and Livvy's heart ached at the thought of losing Nicholas to something as random as a flat tire.

"Dealing with the unexpected is a hallmark of accomplished bakers." Taylor scanned the groups, landing on Nicholas and David in the middle. "In a rush at the restaurant, you find yourself without the ingredient you wanted to use. Something happens to render your equipment unusable. Maybe an assistant walks out on you or fails to show up for work.

"Whatever the circumstance, you have to roll with the punches. You two were punched hard today with a situation no one could have seen coming. And while it was a valiant effort, it simply wasn't enough to escape the elimination round."

Adeline also swept over the groups with her gaze, but Livvy's heart pounded as she stopped on her and Evan.

"Before we dismiss the remaining two groups to make their way to the viewing area, I want to congratulate Livvy and Evan.

Your out-of-the-box thinking in taking your motorcycle added much-needed baking time. With the extra minutes, you two were able to turn out not only a beautiful cake but also one with perfectly paired flavors, expertly done from beginning to end."

Livvy didn't try to contain her grin as she looked up at Evan. His smile mirrored her happiness, and a blush flooded her cheeks as he took her hand. She resisted the urge to tug it away as she caught Adeline's raised eyebrow. Instead, she nodded her thanks to the judges and moved with Evan, Will, and Harper to the viewing area.

Watching Nicholas and David move to their stations, Livvy sobered. She understood the rules, and she realized unexpected things happened every day. She hated for anyone to go to elimination. No, that wasn't entirely true. Will could go anytime, and she'd be just fine. Of course, he always managed to escape that fate. Was it skill, luck, or something a bit sinister that kept him safely in the viewing area during each elimination?

There was no time to come to a satisfactory answer before Taylor announced the beginning of the elimination round. Nicholas and David flew into action. Throughout the ninety-minute challenge, Livvy worried her hands together. She had nothing against David, but she wasn't prepared to say her goodbyes to Nicholas. Was it wrong to pray he'd be able to stay?

13

Livvy struggled to keep her balance as Harper grabbed her arm and yanked her from the hallway when she walked by. She pushed away the hand gripping her and sucked in a deep breath through her nose, releasing it through her mouth. It wouldn't do to be rude to her friend just because suspicious thoughts were stressing her out.

"Is there something I can do for you, Harper?"

Harper stuck her head out the door and looked both ways down the hall before shutting the door, then crossed to the far side of the room and motioned for Livvy to follow.

"Very cloak and dagger."

"Make fun all you want, but something is going on around here." Harper crossed her arms across her chest.

"What do you mean?" She ignored the dread at hearing her thoughts echoed. "David lost the elimination fair and square. I hate that he and Nicholas even ended up there, but I understand why the judges had to do it."

"It's not just that. Don't you find it strange that their tire had a nail in it?"

She lifted a shoulder. "That car visits the studio lot every day.

It probably came from an area where they're building or tearing down a set. Things happen."

"You don't believe that any more than I do." Harper stared at her. "There are too many things happening to be coincidences. And for it to happen to Nicholas after his run-in with Will last night ..."

"You mean that dust-up they were talking about when we were assigned our partners? It was nothing."

"I'm not stupid." Harper's lips pursed. "I spoke with Daniel. He told me he saw the tapes from the house cameras last night. Honestly, I'm surprised Will doesn't have a mark across his face."

Livvy covered her face and groaned. They were warned about the cameras being stationed in all the living areas, but since they were hidden, it was easy to forget they were there. Everyone on the crew had probably seen her slap Will by now. What hope did she have that it wouldn't end up on national television?

Her head snapped up as her breaths came shallow and quick. "What else did Daniel tell you about last night?"

"Nothing much." Harper's sheepish grin told Livvy what she wanted to know before her words. "Except he did say something about you and a certain gorgeous guy locking lips last night. Is it true? You and Evan?"

As she tried to think through all the conversations she'd had with the other competitors, she groaned down to her toes. How much personal information had she shared? There weren't cameras in bathrooms or bedrooms, but they were everywhere else, including the patio and pool area. What was America going to see when they tuned in for this season of *Cake That*?

"I knew it! I've wondered about you two from the beginning. You're so lucky. He's so sweet, and the way he tries to protect you from Will is so cute. You've got to tell me everything. Is he a good kisser?"

Livvy held up her hands. "No. No, I do not have to tell you everything. There's hardly anything to tell. We've not even talked about it yet."

"Well?"

"Well, what?"

"How was it?"

As much as she wanted to ignore the question, Livvy couldn't help but smile. She hoped she didn't sound as dreamy as she felt. "It was amazing."

"I knew it!" Harper squealed. "And I'm so happy for you. Jealous for me of course, but not even really jealous. I mean, I have Daniel. We can't say anything until after taping, but he hinted that he likes me and wants to stay in touch after the show. Oh, we could both come out of this with the love of our lives."

"Slow down there, Sparky. Evan and I kissed. We're not picking out china. We both have a competition requiring our concentration. As for you and Daniel, I thought you were putting a stop to that. It's against the rules."

Harper blushed but was otherwise unrepentant. "I know, but that's precisely why we're careful. He can't kiss me, of course. He can't even hold my hand, but we both know we want to. Kiss, I mean. It's only a matter of time. The show won't last forever. Besides, how would I have known about you and Evan or Will and Nicholas without Daniel telling me? You certainly didn't rush up here to tell me. Hmm."

"Hmm, what?"

"The way Nicholas took up for you, I'd almost say he's got a thing for you, too." Harper shook her head. "But he's too old."

"And I'm his daughter's age. He looks at me like a daughter."

"Daughter or not, he should be careful. According to Daniel, he really got on Will's bad side last night. And I've noticed where there's trouble with Will, there's trouble in the competition."

Again, her own concerns were being voiced. "Are you thinking Will is somehow responsible for these accidents?"

Harper shrugged. "It does seem like an awfully big coincidence that he's been part of every bad thing that's happened during the show. And he is so competitive. I asked Daniel to talk to the higher-ups about it."

"Is he going to?"

"No." She shook her head. "He said there's not enough evidence to prove the incidents aren't accidents, much less link them to Will. Besides, I don't think he meshes well with the other crew members."

"What makes you say that?"

"He's an intern. Even though *Cake That* was his idea, they still treat him like an intern. He's tried to prove himself to them, but they can't even be bothered to call him by his full name. They wouldn't take him seriously if he did go to them. But one day, he's going to show all of them just how important he is to the show."

"I know you believe you know what you're doing, but you should be careful with Daniel." Livvy frowned. "I'd hate for you to get into trouble."

"Don't worry about me. Watch out for yourself. If Will finds out you and Evan were kissing, I bet you two will be the next contestants with bulls-eyes on your backs."

That was the last thing Livvy wanted. Maybe they were wrong about Will. They could be wrong, right? He was an egotistical competitor, but would he stoop to sabotage? The misfortunes happening around him seemed to bring him great pleasure, but did that mean he instigated them? She would have to keep her eyes and ears open in the coming days.

Later in the evening, after the group finished supper and made their way to the hot tub, she was still lost in thought about the possibility of sabotage. She and Evan opted to sit on the patio instead, close enough to be part of the group but far enough to have a private conversation if they wanted. Well, maybe not so private. She wouldn't forget about the hidden cameras as easily from now on.

"Don't like hot tubs?" Evan interrupted her thoughts.

"Not really, at least not when it's already hot outside." She looked at the others soaking in the warm water. "I want something to cool me off, not boil me like a lobster. You?"

"They're all right, but you seem preoccupied tonight." He slid his chair closer. "Besides, I wanted to talk to you without everyone else hanging around. It's hard to find a time to have you to myself."

She blushed and looked away. The smile playing with the corners of her lips faded as her gaze collided with Will's cold stare from the corner of the hot tub. He'd seen the exchange even if he couldn't hear what Evan said. Pulling himself from the hot tub, he stalked inside. Evan seemed oblivious to the waves of anger surging off Will as he made his way past them.

"I'm not sure you should be saying things like that."

He sat up straight beside her. She'd seen Will make him angry and protective with his horrible behavior. This look was different, and she couldn't quite place it. Was he upset with her? Uncomfortable?

"So, you think last night was a mistake." His voice was flat when he spoke, giving no indication of his thoughts.

It wasn't a question, but Livvy felt compelled to respond. "I just think there are people who might take issue with your attention toward me."

"I don't care what Will thinks." His jaw tightened as he glared in the direction of the hot tub and then the patio door. "If I want to give you attention, I can. If I wanted to kiss you again, I certainly wouldn't need his approval to do so."

"*If* you wanted to kiss me again?" Livvy felt sick. "Are you saying you don't?"

He winced, and Livvy couldn't hide a frown. Apparently, that little piece of information was supposed to remain a secret. She was sure of it. Had he simply gotten lost in the moment when he kissed her? Was that the off feeling she'd experienced throughout the day? Evan wasn't that type of person. He would only kiss someone he cared about, right?

Had he not enjoyed the kiss as much as she had? What was it about her that made men perpetually friendzone her?

"It's fine, Evan." She rose before the tears stinging her eyes could fall. "I understand. I'm not going to push it. We'll be friends, and we'll finish the competition. Then, we'll go back to our separate lives. I'm just sorry that my first kiss was a mistake that will more than likely be broadcast across the United States."

"You mean our first kiss."

"No, I mean *my* first kiss. Ever. Not just on the show. Not just between us. And now I'll get to relive both the high and the low every time the episode airs. I've got to go." She couldn't hide the tears any longer. As quickly as she could without drawing attention, she fled inside to the sanctuary of her room.

EVAN RESTED his elbows on his knees and dropped his head into his hands. Her first kiss? Sure, she'd talked about her scarce dating life, but all women thought things like that. If he was her first kiss, then the things Will kept insinuating had to hit doubly hard. Of course, all Will did was talk. He hadn't kissed her, hadn't unintentionally led her on. Which was worse?

"I'm going to assume you cleared things up with Livvy."

"Yep." Evan didn't raise his head as Nicholas claimed the seat Livvy had vacated.

"And it didn't go over well?"

Evan groaned. He didn't need an 'I told you so.' But he deserved one, and so much more. Given Nicholas's care for Livvy, Evan expected fury. Currently, he seemed less angry and more matter-of-fact. But the whole story had yet to come out, and all it would take was speaking with Livvy to get the details. Might as well lay it out there himself and get the tongue lashing over with sooner rather than later.

"It was her first kiss. I didn't know."

A sigh emanated from the man beside him. "I wondered.

Livvy has been very sheltered in many ways. The men in her life have been content to have her as a friend."

"How is that possible?"

"I'm sure there have been men who wanted more, but I guess Livvy never saw it or gave them encouragement to try. She made a self-fulfilling prophecy that colored her perceptions of herself. And it makes her current situation hurt even worse."

Evan didn't need to be told that any more than he needed a reminder that he'd been warned and shrugged it off. The idea that he'd hurt Livvy twisted his insides into knots. But as much as he'd like to make things right, it was better this way. For both of them.

Neither needed the distraction from their goals. Win or lose —and one would have to lose for the other to win—it should happen because of their baking abilities, not because their heads were stuck in a cloud of romance. Now he only had to find a way to get both Livvy and his heart on board with his logic.

14

Livvy felt the pressure the moment she stepped into the studio. There was a strange energy in the atmosphere as she entered the building. There was always tension; with ten people battling to be called the *Cake That* champion baker and win one hundred thousand dollars, every day offered up a great deal of tension.

The set was no stranger to creative energy, either. Each competitor needed that in spades for a chance at the title and prize money. This was an entirely different feeling, and it left Livvy unsettled.

Maybe it was just her. Last night was less than stellar, finding out one more time what she'd known all along. She was friend material but not relationship material. She shouldn't have entertained the thought of being more, especially to a man like Evan. It left her heartbroken and restless when she should have been sleeping peacefully to recharge for the day's competition.

She glanced to where Evan stood at the other side of their dwindling group. He seemed tense as well. Come to think of it, the others seemed a little on edge, and they weren't involved in the drama between her and Evan. The energy she felt must not be about them after all. But if not, what was it?

Crew members were on the outside edges of the competition every day. At first, Livvy had been distracted as she watched them come and go, carrying out various tasks for the show's taping, but lately they'd blended in like they were part of the scenery.

Today, several engaged in whispered conversations before racing to their next task, and Livvy found them impossible to overlook. What was going on? Could Harper be correct in her suspicions of sabotage? Why else would things feel so unlike the previous days of competition?

"Good morning." Rhonda stepped in front of them, barring their entry onto the set. "I trust you all had a good night and are ready for another exciting day in the *Cake That* kitchen." Her quick intake of breath didn't leave time for response. It wasn't meant to. "We have a surprise for you today, which I believe you're going to love." She motioned to Daniel, who came to stand beside her.

"However, before you go in, Danny is going to escort you to the reaction room for some quick interviews. I know we usually do them after each taping. Today we will do a before and after. Danny?"

He forced a smile past the tightness in his jaw. "Thank you, Rhonda." He motioned down the hall with a sweep of his hand. "Please follow me."

Before Livvy fell dutifully in line behind the others, she stole a glance at Harper. She might think she was being careful to hide her relationship with Daniel, but one look at her face would alert any onlookers to the truth. Her indignation at Rhonda's flippancy was clear evidence of how taken she was with him.

If there was any privacy, Livvy had no doubt Harper would have run to him to soothe his wounded pride. At least she was exercising some restraint. Maybe it would be enough to protect her.

Livvy took a seat in one of the chairs lined up outside the reaction room. It was the same after every taping. They sat.

They waited. They spilled their guts on camera about all the surprises, disappointments, and frustrations of the day. They went home. But nothing had happened yet. What subject could they possibly find to use for a decent interview?

Each interview lasted only a few short minutes. As she walked back toward the set, Livvy wondered at the usefulness of the information they'd gleaned from each contestant. If everyone's interviews were like hers, all the crew received was background information that was readily available in their audition videos.

It had been difficult enough to explain her family situations in her audition. They had wanted to discuss it again. She felt thrown off her game after having to rehash her loss and the role her friends now occupied as family to fill the empty spaces in her life. With the pool of competitors shrinking every day, she couldn't afford to be less than her best in the kitchen. Could that possibly be their plan?

Something was definitely up. Taylor and Adeline were standing behind the judges' table with conspiratorial grins on their faces.

"Welcome back." Adeline clasped her hands in front of her. "I know you're all anxious to find out about the surprise twist in today's show. We won't keep you in suspense any longer."

Taylor placed his hands on the back of his chair and raised his voice. "Send out our surprise."

Every competitor turned toward movement at the judges' entrance. Livvy watched as, one by one, people she'd never met came through the door and were greeted with laughter, hugs, and even a squeal from Harper, as she enveloped an older version of herself in her arms. The woman with Nicholas had to be Isabel. No one else would provoke the sheen of tears she saw.

Will exchanged a handshake and shoulder slap combo with a man who could have been his twin. Evan rushed toward the small woman coming from the door and scooped her up in a jubilant hug, barely refraining from swinging her around. Livvy had only just decided they shared the same eyes when she caught sight of Tabitha coming quietly into the room.

Livvy rushed her even as she knew the whole experience had to petrify her socially anxious best friend. But she was here, and that was all that mattered. She threw her arms around her and whispered, "I'm so glad you're here! I have so much to tell you."

Tabitha pulled back and smiled as if she were waiting for something. But what? Livvy looked her over from head to toe and back to the top of her head again before it hit her.

"You did it! I can't believe you worked up the nerve, but I couldn't be happier." She fingered the bow of the hot pink and black polka-dotted headband Tabitha had worn for the occasion. "It looks great on you. Before you know it, you'll be the life of the party."

"I better not be." Tabitha blanched. "I'll don the headband and the apron for you just this once. You can keep the crowds and parties, thank you very much."

A look from the judges ended thoughts of continuing the conversation. Livvy moved into place with Tabitha at her side. They joined the smiling crowd of competitors and guests in giving all their attention to the duo in front of them.

"No bakers make it on their own." Adeline had taken her seat and folded her hands in front of her. "Somewhere, at some point in their careers, someone has inspired, encouraged, or supported them in some way. Today, we've invited the person we felt fit that description best based on your auditions and interviews."

Taylor moved to take his seat. "Hopefully, your friends and family are as adept in the kitchen as you because you will work in tandem with them to create your cakes. We've not assigned any secret ingredients or planned any twists. Today, you and your guest baker will create a cake that tells us something about your relationship. You have four hours, and your time starts now."

Teams scattered to their workstations. The room filled with the buzz of hurried discussions of strategy before the pairs filled their baskets in the pantry and began work on their cakes.

Daniel and Rhonda conducted mini-interviews with each pair as they returned from the pantry to find out more about the cakes they'd chosen to make. Daniel moved from Livvy and Tabitha's station to the next.

Will's brother was already hard at work on some element of their cake while Will stopped to pick up a notecard from the floor and set it on the counter in Evan's station. Which was worse, having Will sandwiched between her and Evan or the idea that Evan could have been right next to her? Neither was an arrangement she currently relished. But it was what it was. She had a cake to bake and a competition to win.

"I'm not sure what to do first." Tabitha's eyes were wide, and her hands kept flitting from one ingredient to the next without alighting on anything for more than a second.

Livvy's focus shifted from the other stations to her own. Proficient enough in the kitchen, Tabitha had never claimed to be a baker. She'd left Livvy to do what Livvy did best in the kitchen while filling in with the main courses and side dishes. Livvy abandoned her bowl of partially mixed ingredients on the counter and moved to her terrified friend.

Even wanting to be part of the show, Livvy found the lights, cameras, and contests unnerving. Those same elements, combined with Tabitha's reserved nature and fear of failing her best friend, would be a nightmare for her. Livvy grasped her friend's shaking hands. Tabitha looked up, but she couldn't stay focused. She glanced from Livvy to the station beside them to the judges' table and ultimately to the door she'd entered the kitchen through. Livvy smiled. Was she considering running?

"Look at me." She waited until Tabitha made eye contact and kept it. "We are going to do great. You will be amazing, and I couldn't imagine a better partner for today's event."

Tabitha smiled, but Livvy knew her best friend well enough to recognize it was forced.

"You are, after all, wearing my lucky apron." Livvy dropped her hands and straightened the hem.

"They're all your lucky aprons." Tabitha sucked in a deep breath and released a laugh. "But fine. What do I need to do?"

Livvy explained each step, in the order Tabitha would need to follow, before going back to the batter. They worked in companionable silence, each giving their full attention to their tasks. Tabitha's shoulders relaxed as she got lost in the assignments, and they quickly made up the lost time.

"Coming behind." Livvy made sure the other competitors heard before she made her way behind their stations. She hurried past Will and his brother, hoping to avoid the same type of incident that had cost Emma so much. They were so intent on their work they didn't seem to notice her. As she slid her cakes into the ovens behind Evan and his mother, work at their station came to a halt.

"I'm not sure what happened, and I have no idea how to fix it."

"Did you follow the recipe I wrote out exactly?" Evan swiped the beanie from his head and tossed it on the counter.

Tears welled in the older woman's eyes. "Of course, I did. Four egg yolks, three cups sugar, one tablespoon lemon zest ..."

"Wait." He took the card from her hand. "I didn't write this. I wrote a two-thirds cup of sugar, not three cups. Look at this. It's erased. Who could have done that?"

"I don't know." She shook her head. "The only time I didn't have it was when we went to the pantry. I am so sorry, Evan."

"It doesn't matter." He glanced in Will's direction before reassuring his mother. "It's not your fault, and we can still salvage this. You up for it?"

She nodded and grabbed a clean bowl from under the counter. Evan's tight-lipped grin as he looked at Livvy revealed the stress he felt. They didn't have time for elements to fail, but he wanted to protect his mom's feelings. It was a noble gesture, but she wouldn't have expected anything less from him. It was just one of the many things about him that she'd found attractive.

Oh, who was she kidding? She was still completely over the moon for him, and that was the problem. With one kiss, he'd given her hope. With one admission of regret, he'd taken it back. She looked away and hurried back to her station before he saw more truth in her eyes than she wanted to show.

"Drama down at that end?" Tabitha jerked her head in their direction.

"We're just friends."

Tabitha quirked an eyebrow. No additional questions were voiced, but they didn't have to be for Livvy to realize her mistake. She rummaged through the ingredients on the counter as if nothing was amiss.

"I think it was something about an incorrect recipe, but I'm sure it will be fine."

"Got it."

The look Livvy received assured her Tabitha did get it. She probably understood far more than Livvy wanted her to but would also wait for a more opportune time to revisit the subject. That was fine. They had a lot of work to do and little time to do it.

Working side by side with Tabitha made the minutes slip by quicker than she expected. They added the last crumbles of graham cracker to the frosting as Taylor called for the competitors to cease work. Livvy hoped they wouldn't ship their guests out as soon as the judging ended. A talk with Tabitha was overdue, but for now, she had to focus on presenting their cake and cupcakes. She picked up the tray and moved to the judges' table.

Adeline smiled her polite judge's smile. "Livvy, can you introduce us to your guest and tell us about your cake and cupcakes?"

Hands out to her side like a game show model showing off the grand prize, Livvy gave Tabitha the introduction she deserved but probably didn't appreciate. "This is my best friend and roommate, Tabitha. After my parents and later my grandmother passed away, her family became my family. She's the one who encouraged me to audition for *Cake That*, and she's my biggest cheerleader.

"We met at a summer camp the year her family moved into town. Sharing s'mores around the campfire is one of our first memories together, and that is why we have a s'mores-inspired cake for you today."

Tabitha fidgeted while the judges ate in silence. The nervous energy reminded Livvy of the first day of competition. It was strange that it took seeing the competition through the eyes of her friend to realize how comfortable she'd become with all the show's trappings. As they returned to the group, Evan and his mother stepped forward.

After the introductions, Evan explained their creation. "Mom was never much of a baker when I was growing up, but it didn't keep her from trying. When I was a sophomore, my class hosted a bake sale for our end-of-year trip. Mom decided to make lemon bars. By the time I got home, the kitchen was a total wreck, and a pan of lemon bars was burnt beyond recognition.

"It was a disaster, and Mom was upset, but we decided to try again. This time we did it together. They were amazing, and it's one of my favorite memories with my mom in the kitchen. It's why we chose to make a lemon cake with lemon curd filling for you today."

"It seems you had some issues with your recipe." It was no surprise for Taylor to bring up the incident. "Would you care to elaborate?"

"I wrote the recipe for the lemon curd on a notecard before we went to the pantry." Evan cleared his throat. "I knew Mom would need it, and I told her to follow it exactly while I prepared the cake batter. I must have miswritten it, and the extra sugar rendered the curd unusable. We made a new one, but it didn't have time to set up like we wanted."

As Evan took the blame for the card, his mother reached for

his hand. He didn't believe it, but he wasn't going to cause a scene. Though she acted like she wanted to say something, Evan squeezed his mom's hand and gave a slight shake of his head. The idea that someone tampered with the card wouldn't be brought up by him or anyone else during the judging. With all the other drama, Livvy understood his desire to avoid adding more. Evan's mother had raised a good man.

He accepted his place in the elimination round with the same spirit he'd shown when questioned about the recipe error. While his mother watched from the viewing area, he would bake to save himself. Harper looked like she might be sick as the judges sentenced her to the same fate. Evan was a worthy opponent, and they'd both previously faced the elimination round, negating any advantage due to experience.

Whoever won, it would be based solely on their creations.

15

The laughter around the table at dinner that night was stilted and uncomfortable. No matter what lighthearted subject they discussed, a thread of tension remained. The guests of the four remaining competitors could stay until midnight, and they were making the most of their time, sharing stories and getting to know the others around the table.

"Tell me something, Livvy." Will's brother, Derrick, cut into his steak as he looked across the table. "How is it my brother hasn't snagged you yet? You're a beautiful woman, and you seem smart. I'm sure you've found out by now he's the most eligible man in the room."

Livvy choked on her water. Tabitha's fork clattered against her plate. On the other side of her, Evan shifted in the seat, opened his mouth, but shut it without saying a word. The gesture was enough to draw attention without helping the situation.

"So, that's how it is?" Derrick raised an eyebrow. "I guess you're not as smart as I thought you were."

How could there be two of them in the same room? Livvy's cheeks burned even as she glared at the man across the table. As if dealing with Will wasn't hard enough. And now, it would seem she'd lost the ally she'd once had in Evan. But there were only a few hours left, and dinner was almost over.

"Papa tells me you and I would get along well." Isabel spoke to Livvy from her place next to Nicholas, breaking the tense silence. "That we're very much alike."

It was a lifeline, and she was going to take it. "I'd love the opportunity to get to know you. Your father has had such wonderful things to say about you, I feel I know you already."

"Maybe you can come for a visit sometime after the show airs. I know my papa would enjoy that."

"Where are you from, Isabel?" Tabitha leaned around Livvy.

"I was born in California, but we've lived in Arizona since I was six years old."

Livvy swallowed a bite of her salad. "Arizona? I've heard the summer temperatures soar out that way."

"The temperatures can be very high." Isabel nodded. "But it's a different heat than you're used to in St. Louis. You have humidity. I've visited in the summer, and some days the air felt so thick I didn't think I'd be able to get a breath. The heat in Arizona is just heat. It makes a difference."

Everyone's attention was diverted to places they'd lived and visited. Will and Derrick, of course, knew something about every place mentioned, but at least the conversation didn't come back to her for the rest of the meal. Shortly after loading their dishes into the dishwasher, everyone went their separate ways for time alone with their guests. While some wandered into the game room or outside to the pool, Livvy led Tabitha up to her room. It was time for a talk.

Cross-legged on the bed facing each other like when they had junior high sleepovers, Livvy jumped into the conversation she'd been dying to have since Tabitha walked onto the set that morning. "You would not believe what has happened the week we've been here."

"And I'm ready to hear everything. I couldn't have ignored the sparks if I'd wanted to."

Livvy scrunched up her face. "Sparks? What are you talking about?"

"Don't play dumb with me. Anyone with eyes can see the chemistry between you and Evan. I want to know all about it."

"There's nothing to tell." Livvy shrugged. "At least, not about that. I need to get your input on some odd occurrences that have taken place since filming began."

"Fine, but don't think we aren't going to revisit the subject of your hunky competitor while I'm here."

"Whatever. I'm serious, though. I need you to tell me if my imagination is running wild or if there is something bizarre going on in this competition." Livvy went through each day's events, from Will bumping into Emma on the first day to David and Nicholas's flat tire. "And you saw it today. I know someone had to tamper with Evan's recipe. He wouldn't have made that mistake."

Tabitha rubbed a hand back and forth over her chin. "And you saw Will with the notecard?"

"Yes."

"And he's been involved in almost every disaster?"

"In some way, directly or indirectly. I didn't see him put a nail in the tire of the car, but he is the one who asked not to be paired with Nicholas."

"I don't know, Liv." Tabitha shook her head. "It seems strange the only ones still in the competition who haven't been on the wrong end of these disasters are you and Will. But other than being a complete arrogant jerk, what would his motive be?"

"Will has made it clear from the beginning of the competition that I should be giving him my attention. It's gotten heated."

Tabitha's shoulders tensed. "How heated?"

"One night, he stepped further over the line than simple rudeness, and I slapped him."

"That's pretty heated."

Livvy nodded. "Evan and Nicholas have stood up for me

more than once, and the next day they met with some kitchen disaster. Yesterday, he got angry when Evan and I were having a private conversation that might have seemed a little cozy at first. Today, Evan's recipe was changed. Doesn't that seem a little too coincidental?"

"But you've rebuffed him, and he hasn't come after you."

"I don't know." Livvy shrugged. "Maybe he knows if he does, he'll have zero chance with me. Of course, he has less than that now, but he refuses to accept it."

"Makes sense in a warped way. And I see where it looks like he's targeting the people who stand in his way at getting to you. But do you really think this guy is capable of sabotaging everyone? And you said there weren't any issues on one of the days, right? Why not?"

"I have no answer for either question. It just seems like there's something more than coincidence at play."

"Maybe so, but what I need to know about are the sparks between you and Mr. Hunky."

"Okay. Yes, there were sparks there. But getting kissed by the most gorgeous guy I've ever met ..."

"Oooooh, girl." Tabitha swatted her arm. "You mean to tell me you had your first kiss, and that's not the big important news you want to talk about? I would've led with that news."

"You didn't let me finish." Livvy rolled her eyes. "Getting kissed by him and then told he regrets it can dump some serious water on those sparks."

Tabitha's mouth gaped open. "He did what?"

"It really doesn't matter." Livvy shrugged. "We're here to win a competition, not find our soulmates."

"Maybe so, but who says you can't do both?"

"You could be right. But, like I said, it doesn't matter. Evan didn't even stand up for me at dinner tonight. It's safe to say, even if I haven't gotten over him, he's definitely over me."

"You're not going to get over her that easily. You know that, right?"

Evan took the cup she held out to him and placed it in the cabinet. No one would ever accuse his mother of being less than perceptive. She'd seen through his self-imposed distance from Livvy and coerced the whole story from him while they cleared the table after everyone else moved outside to the pool.

"I never said it would be easy. Livvy's great. She's kindhearted, and funny, and smart. She's a believer, too, and lives it. And we could've been great friends if I'd only stuck with my decision to avoid anything more. Now, there's not much hope for friendship either."

"You're both adults, and from what you told me, she finds you as irresistible as you do her."

He winced as she pinched his cheek.

"And who wouldn't think my handsome boy was the best thing going."

"Mom." He shook his head. "Please. I'm being serious."

"So am I. There's nothing wrong with allowing yourself to get close to someone, especially if she's as great as you're telling me she is."

"Yes, there is. We're in a competition. We're here to win. *I'm* here to win. That's always been the goal, and if I get distracted, that's not going to happen. Then, how will you and dad get your anniversary trip?"

"I want you to listen to me." She sighed as she turned him to face her and cupped his cheeks in her hands. "And hear what I say. Your father and I would love to finally take the trip we've dreamed of since before we were married. But there are things more important to us than that."

"I know, but ..."

Her look and raised hand cut Evan off. "I wasn't done. I know you understand in principle that our family is worth more to us than any trip, but you don't seem to grasp how deeply we feel that."

"I do." Evan removed his beanie and ran a hand through his hair. "That's exactly why I want to be able to do this for you. When you could have been saving for your dream trip, you were using the funds to pay for swimming for me and riding lessons for Tessa and Teressa. You made sure we didn't go without the things we needed when we were kids, and you haven't stopped now. From camps and clubs—"

"To cars and classes?" she grinned up at him.

"—you and Dad have helped us every step of the way. It would mean so much to the three of us to do something for you. To send you on your trip. If I win this, I can make sure that happens."

She took his hands in hers. "And we appreciate how grateful you kids are, but we've not given anything up. Think of all the wonderful memories we've collected over the years. Your swimming and their riding competitions. The joy on your faces when you won. Watching you learn to lose with a winner's attitude. Helping you find the things you're passionate about and letting you pursue them.

"And your dad and I shared each of those times with the person we love more than anything. Each other. We haven't missed out in our married life, and one thing we've always agreed on is that we want our children to find their one to love, as we have.

"I'm not saying we'll never go on our dream trip. But even if we don't, it's okay. God's blessed your father and me beyond our wildest imagination, and we want nothing, not even a trip, more than seeing you and your sisters find those same blessings."

Evan shook his head. "So you're saying give up the competition and get the girl."

"No, son." His mother's smile was the same patient smile he'd received many times as a young boy. "I don't believe you have to give up one to find the other. You can keep chasing the win in the competition. But it's okay if it's not your be-all, end-all. Do your best and have fun. Don't miss out on other opportunities that present themselves because your head is stuck in the sand. Or in the batter, in this case.

"Maybe you came to win, but God wants to give you something more than you bargained for through the competition. Keep your heart and mind open to what He might be offering you. Then you'll win no matter the outcome of the show."

He wrapped his mom in his arms and kissed the top of her head. "Thanks, Mom. I'll keep what you said in mind. It's good to know you won't disown me if I can't win."

"Never over a competition, but if you lose that girl, we might have to talk. She seems like a keeper."

Evan laughed, keeping one arm over her shoulders as they walked to the patio door. "She is, but I may have already burned those bridges beyond my ability to fix them."

"Then we'll ask the Master Carpenter to repair them if He's brought you here for more than the show. Now, let's go get to know your new friends better."

LIVVY STRETCHED her legs out in front of the deck chair she'd claimed by the pool. Spending time with Tabitha was exactly what she'd needed. Even sitting quietly beside her, listening to Isabel's stories about Nicholas as a father, Tabitha brought calm into her world. Getting to know Isabel better was the icing on the cake.

"Don't look now." Tabitha leaned close and spoke for her ears only. "But Mr. Hunky and his mom are headed this way. And his gaze is trained on you like a heat-seeking missile on a jet. It may not be as over as you think."

She rolled her eyes at Tabitha's comparison but couldn't deny the flutter she felt when she glanced in his direction and caught his gaze. Was he watching because he was interested after all? Or maybe he was just scoping out the situation to know if he was welcome. She gave a noncommittal smile before turning her attention back to Isabel and Nicholas. They could occupy the same space and share the same friends, even if there was nothing more between them.

The conversation may have flowed effortlessly over the next hour, but Livvy couldn't deny the ease between her and Evan was gone. Sure, they laughed and talked with everyone else, but even sitting next to each other, the distance between them seemed insurmountable. At least everyone else was there talking and laughing, smoothing over the discomfort without trying.

Isabel nodded at her and Evan. "My Papa has had nothing but wonderful things to say about both of you. I meant my invitation to come visit. We could invite everyone. It could be a reunion of sorts. We have plenty of room."

"That's a wonderful idea." Nicholas took his daughter's hand. "I'll get everyone's information, and we can plan on getting together sometime in the spring before Arizona gets too hot."

They settled their plans just as Daniel and Rhonda came to call an end to the festivities. Once their friends and family were gone, Livvy felt the tension rise in the remaining trio. Nicholas watched them both for a moment before standing.

"I enjoyed tonight, and I'm glad you two were able to set aside whatever is going on between you and have some fun with everyone. But now, you need to deal with it. I'll be in the room if you need me." Nicholas retreated into the house

"Not sure what that was about." Livvy flew to her feet and exaggerated a shrug. "But I think I'll head inside too." She paused when Evan's hand circled her wrist but refused to look at him. "It's fine, Evan. Nicholas is wrong. We don't need to explain anything to each other. We're friends, that's all. What happened was a mistake, and it won't happen again."

He didn't speak, and she fought the urge to look at him.

"Really?" His quiet voice broke the silence. "I was kind of hoping it would."

She glanced at him. A hint of a smile waited to release the

dimples she found so attractive. Even in the dimmed lighting, she could see hope in his eyes. She freed her wrist from his grasp and walked away. What was he doing? It was a mistake, but he hoped it would happen again? What was she supposed to do with that information?

Maybe he would consider it cowardly, but she wasn't prepared to sort through the questions whipping through her mind. With each step she took toward the house, her chest felt tighter. She should turn around. Hashing it out with Evan was the only way to get this thing solved once and for all, but she couldn't. He'd hurt her, and she wasn't emotionally prepared to have a heart-to-heart with him.

Knowing either one of them could be eliminated from the competition in less than twenty-four hours paused her retreat. Of course, there were no guarantees for them even if she turned around now. Evan hadn't said kissing her wasn't a mistake, only that he might like it to happen again. She had no idea what to do with that. No. It was better to leave things as they were.

Livvy continued into the house and up to her room without glancing at the man she was leaving behind.

16

Adeline scanned the quartet of contestants standing before her. "This is the last round of regular competition before we mix things up for the semi-finals."

Her show smile did nothing to calm the jitters her words evoked. Livvy wrung her hands together. She'd made it to the final four. She was only a few days of competition away from paying off the debt on The Sugar Cube. Providing, of course, she didn't get eliminated between now and then.

"What better way to shake up the day than adding a guest judge to the party?" Taylor spoke as he rose from his chair and made his way to the doorway their family and friends had used during the previous taping. His arm swung wide toward the door to draw their attention to the man entering.

No. It couldn't be. Parker Kelly was their guest judge! An audible gasp escaped before Livvy could contain it. Heat flooded her cheeks as Taylor laughed.

"I see at least one of you is familiar with Mr. Parker Kelly. His world-famous bakery, Frosted, is located right here in Los Angeles. He's won every cake decorating award possible and been the focus of multiple magazine spreads and television interviews. And he is our guest judge for this final round before the semi-final competition begins."

If *dapper* were still used in everyday speech, Livvy would pair it with *unconventional* to sum up the man standing before them. He was nearing his sixties, but though his slightly graying blonde hair was kept close-cropped to disguise its thinness, he presented himself with the ease of youth.

Livvy was surprised to find he was only, at most, an inch taller than her. His gray suit was fitted to his narrow form and accented with a purple pocket square and polka-dotted bow tie. His eyes crinkled behind his thin wire-rimmed round glasses as he smiled and offered a small wave.

"Adeline and Taylor have kept me apprised of your work, and I must say I'm impressed. You four have shown tenacity and talent throughout the competition. In honor of those qualities, I've planned a field trip for you. Today you will be my guests for a behind-the-scenes tour of Frosted before your competition."

"Cut," the director's voice called out after the cameras had a chance to capture the contestants' reactions.

"Today's show is going to require some production magic." Rhonda stepped forward from behind the lighting and camera crew. "While the episode will air as if your trip to Frosted and your competition take place on the same day, that is simply not feasible. Filming for this episode will take place today and tomorrow.

"You've made it this far in the competition and deserve a break for the day. We will film your trip and a few reaction segments today, and tomorrow we will gather for the competition portion of the episode. Dan will fill you in on the important details."

Daniel's jaw was set as he took Rhonda's place in front of them. His eyes followed her path momentarily before he turned his focus back to his task and forced a smile. "One of the show cars will take all four of you to Mr. Kelly's bakery as soon as you're dismissed. Mr. Kelly will meet you there, though Taylor and Adeline will not be in attendance. After touring Frosted, reaction videos will be taped on location before you return to the house.

"Tomorrow, taping will resume as usual. However, we ask you to please remember to wear the same outfits you're wearing today. We want the tapings to flow together as if they were done in one day. Thank you. You are dismissed."

Livvy grabbed Nicholas's arm as Evan climbed into the waiting vehicle. "I can't believe we get to visit Frosted and that Parker Kelly will give us a tour himself!"

Before he could answer, Will cut in. "I doubt it's everything the shows and magazines make it out to be. I mean, the man has talent as a decorator, but is what he turns out that far above everyone else?"

"Of course, you would say that." Nicholas scoffed at Will's back as he climbed into the car. "You cannot believe anyone could be as brilliant in the kitchen as yourself."

"You think I'm brilliant? Finally, someone other than myself shows a little taste." Will looked directly at her and Evan as he spoke.

Why couldn't he act like a grown man and deal with the fact that she'd been less than interested? Livvy sighed as she took a seat beside Evan and across from Nicholas and Will, forced a tight smile, and looked out the window. He clearly didn't know about the rift in her relationship with Evan.

She practically jumped when Evan's hand found hers with an encouraging squeeze. Maybe he wasn't aware of their issues either. Or maybe he was just playing a part to keep Will at bay. He'd placed himself between her and Will several times before their kiss. Why should he stop now? Just because they were not meant to be together didn't mean he wouldn't help her deal with Will's unwanted attention.

An awkward silence descended over the remainder of the

ride, but some of the heaviness dissipated as she got her first look at Frosted. Videos and pictures in magazine spreads didn't do the trendy bakery justice. Huge windows framed the door on both sides, giving the perfect view of the interior to draw in those passing by.

Mr. Kelly met them at the door and ushered them inside. Camera crews were already in position in out-of-the-way places. Livvy breathed in the aroma of vanilla and sugar that seemed to permeate bakeries. It always felt like home.

Warm-toned wood counters trimmed in sleek black complemented the brick walls. The sparse shelves and frames mounted on the walls matched the black of the countertops. Copper light fixtures and accent pieces were scattered throughout the room. It was tasteful and rustically elegant, letting the artistry of Parker Kelly's cakes be the focal point of the room.

Being on *Cake That* was a dream come true in itself. But standing in Frosted, waiting for Parker Kelly to give her a tour, bumped the actual competition from its place as the most amazing thing she'd ever experienced. No matter how many years she had ahead of her, she would never forget this day.

Mr. Kelly allowed them to explore the front of the bakery. He patiently answered questions about the shop itself and drank in their praise of its design before ushering them into the kitchen.

He took his place behind a row of undecorated cakes perched on a stainless-steel table. Tools of the cake decorating trade were laid out, ready for use. Every surface of the work area gleamed under the lights. Mr. Kelly's kitchen was spotless.

"Many elements of cake decorating have evolved throughout the years. New techniques are in constant development. Styles come and go with the seasons. However, one thing never changes: only those with the heart of an artist will rise to the top in the field of cake decorating.

"Skills can be mastered, colors can be matched, and elements balanced through practice. But technical proficiency is not true artistry. And those who stand out among their peers as cake decorators have an artist's heart, a natural leaning to beauty and form that shows in everything they create."

Mr. Kelly described his process, from using discussions with his clients to get a feel for their personalities to incorporating the information into the design of each cake to tailor it to the individual.

"Sometimes, I have to get creative. If you've seen any of my shows, you'll know the one thing we don't use is nuts or nut butters, including peanut butter, in any of our cakes. I have nut allergies, and they, along with peanut allergies, are very common. I want everyone to be able to enjoy what my shop has to offer.

"Because of this, I made the conscious choice to push myself beyond peanut and nut-based flavor profiles. I have to bring something even better to the table. Each creation is your opportunity to go beyond the mundane."

He regaled them with stories of his struggles and successes while decorating the cake in front of him. By the time he finished speaking, the cake was fully decorated. Livvy was shocked at how quickly he was able to create the masterpiece.

Marbled gray and white fondant covered the cake, giving a classic, elegant look to build on. He had added mauve and buttery yellow ribbon and floral accents for pops of color. It was straightforward and tasteful, like everything else in Frosted.

"This cake is a representation of me. As I decorated it, I thought only of my own likes and desires. When I create for others, I consider their style and wishes, but I never fail to put a piece of myself into the design. Incorporating my heart into each order is what transforms their cake into a Parker Kelly cake. It sets me apart. Find out who you are, and don't be afraid to set yourself apart by allowing who you are to shine through in each cake you make."

Livvy considered his words. She poured her heart and soul into her business. Did she also pour it into each individual creation? It felt like she did. She hoped it was true. The day creating her cupcakes turned into an assembly line was the day she'd hang up her polka-dotted apron.

"Now, if everyone will claim a space to work, it's time to get your hands dirty. I'd like everyone to recreate my cake. If you have any questions, don't hesitate to ask."

Livvy chose the free cake at the end of the counter and got to work. Evan worked beside her with Nicholas next to him and Will at the far end of the table. As they worked, conversation flowed as smoothly as the frosting spread across their blank sponge canvases. Even Will's contributions to the discussions were friendlier. It was refreshing, and Livvy entered her creative zone with ease.

Before she realized it, an hour passed, and everyone worked to put the finishing touches on their cakes. Livvy compared hers to Parker Kelly's cake and decided she'd done a creditable job recreating it. Of course, it was a fairly simple design without many advanced techniques, but making a Parker Kelly cake with accuracy gave her a sense of accomplishment. She stole a glance at the other cakes, deciding they were as well executed as her own.

All the competitors she'd gone against were great bakers, but these three were of the highest quality. Even Will's talent couldn't be denied, though part of her hated to admit it.

Mr. Kelly examined each cake. "Beautiful work. I can't wait to see what you create during tomorrow's competition."

His praise kept Livvy smiling to the car and all the way back to the studio to tape the reaction videos. She'd followed his career from the time he started gaining notoriety. His rise to stardom seemed instantaneous. However, from hearing his story today, she recognized the hard work and dedication that had gone into his career before anyone knew his name.

Hope welled inside her as she began to realize what she'd seen as setbacks and slow progress might be more normal than she'd thought. And if she managed to win *Cake That*, it could put her on the fast track to The Sugar Cube becoming everything she'd dreamed.

17

"I don't know what everyone's fascination is with Parker Kelly." Livvy rolled her eyes. "Don't pretend, Will. You were as enamored with Frosted as everyone else."

Stretched out on one of the sofas, he waved a hand in her direction as if shooing off a pesky fly. "I was simply being polite. Whether or not I think he's as great as everyone says, he is the guest judge for tomorrow's competition. I know the win will be easy, no offense to anyone here, but I'm not going to sabotage my chances by alienating the guest judge. If he turns against me, it won't matter how good I am." His choice of words hung heavy in the air like toxic fog.

How could he even say sabotage without considering he was on a shortlist of those who might be working against his fellow competitors? Either he was convinced no one would find out what he was doing, or he was as innocent as the rest of them.

"Whatever you say, Will." Livvy shook her head. "I still think you were more impressed than you let on, but I'm not going to argue the point. I, for one, adored Frosted. It's even more gorgeous in person than on television. And if you could bottle the scents mingling in the air when you open the door, you could make millions. It would make any place a home away from home."

Will looked bored. She doubted he ever allowed himself to take comfort in a scent and wondered if he knew the sense of peace that home could offer. Such things were obviously beneath him, and he wasn't afraid to make that abundantly clear to the rest of the group. Livvy didn't let him derail her enthusiasm. Instead, she looked to Evan and Nicholas.

"I can't say much about the aromas." Nicholas took a sip from the steaming cup of coffee in his hand. "I noticed them, but they didn't impact me the way they did you. Maybe it's one of those things that generally mean more to you than others. I did enjoy his shop. Mr. Kelly has a level of expertise and success that anyone can appreciate."

Evan handed her a mug of cocoa before settling on the sofa beside her with his own steaming cup. Earthy scents of cinnamon and nutmeg blended with orange momentarily replaced the rich smell of chocolate as steam from his tea wafted her direction. It seemed he would keep up the pretense of their relationship to keep Will at arm's length. She leaned back against the sofa cushion, careful not to jostle her drink.

"I think I missed part of the conversation, but if we're discussing Frosted, I think Nicholas is right. I came away more impressed with the man and his empire than I have ever felt watching him on television or reading about him in magazines. I completely understand why the producers chose him as a guest judge."

Will lifted his head from the back of the loveseat he reclined on. "Any idea what they're going to make us do for our challenge tomorrow?"

"They've made us throw darts at giant maps of the world." Livvy snorted and quickly slapped a hand over her mouth. Too late to salvage any ideas that she could be ladylike, she didn't even try. "I can't imagine what will be next. Cake decorating while dangling from a bungee cord?"

"I doubt it will be anything as dramatic as that." Evan shook his head. "Though I have to admit I'd watch that show. I've tried to pick apart everything that happened today to figure it out, but I still have no idea."

Nicholas shrugged. "No guesses from me either."

"I guess we'll have to wait until tomorrow to find out." Will looked at each of them. "Think about it, though. By the end of the day tomorrow, one of you will be sent home. Our little group will be down to three, and I will be that much closer to winning one hundred thousand dollars."

The look he gave Livvy made her lips tighten.

"There's still time if you want to find out what it's like to be with a winner. I guarantee I can show you a better time than the choir boy with all his chaste kisses and junior high hand-holding."

Evan moved to stand, but Livvy laid a hand on his arm. The muscles were tense under her fingers. From previous run-ins with Will, she knew Evan's jaw would be tight and his eyes telegraphing his displeasure. But she refused to look and, in doing so, release Will from the brunt of the glare she focused on him. From the corner of her eye, she saw Nicholas shift but remain seated, taking his cue from her.

"For a moment, I almost forgot how disgusting and inappropriate you can be." Her voice was full of ice despite the anger pulsing through her veins. "I thought we might start getting along. But one little opportunity, and you slipped right back into the Will we've seen every other day. I hate to say it, but I hope you're eliminated tomorrow.

"I've tried to be patient, but I'm not going to have you speaking like that and insinuating things about me anymore. Whether you are eliminated or not, this stops tonight. You have no chance with me. Time to move on."

Will leaned back against the sofa cushions. Probably trying to appear unfazed by her words, but a flash in his eyes told her she'd hit the mark. He didn't like what she said and was embarrassed. Too bad he'd never admit it and let all of them get past this. His arm stretched along the back of the loveseat for a moment before he brought his fist up and rested his head against it.

"As you said earlier, I'm not going to argue my point with you. We both know there have been enough sparks between us to light up a football stadium. But for whatever reason, you've settled for less. Evan won't be here forever. In fact, there's a good chance tonight's your last night with him."

Before anyone could comment, Will stood and walked from the room. Livvy sat in silence, staring at the empty doorway.

"He just can't accept it." Livvy turned to Nicholas. "I'm not sure why I even try."

"No. You have to keep trying because Will is right about one very important fact."

"What's that?"

"One of us is going home tomorrow. If it's Will, the problem is taken care of by itself. The same is true if it's you. If I go, you've still got Evan with you. If Evan goes, I don't know that a father figure will be enough to persuade someone as egotistical as Will to focus his attentions somewhere far from you."

Evan shook his head. "Nicholas is right. Whether Will wants to believe it or not, you've got to keep telling him you're not interested. It wouldn't hurt to have a plan on where to turn if things get out of hand, too."

"Things have already gotten out of hand with him."

"No. Things have not gotten nearly as out of hand as they could." Nicholas frowned. "I don't like to think badly of anyone, but Will could get physical, especially without Evan as a deterrent. Now, don't look at me like that. I don't mean I think he'd stoop to assault. I can, however, see him encroaching on your space and pushing boundaries. As much as I'd do anything to protect you, I'm not as formidable to him as Evan."

"There are cameras everywhere. I'm sure if he tries anything, the people running the show will put a stop to it, right?"

"They've not done much about any of the problems on the show, whether they happen at the house or during competition." Evan shrugged. "Drama is good for ratings."

Livvy bit her lip. She couldn't argue with him. There had been too many strange occurrences to be a coincidence. No one on the production team had lifted a finger to set things right. And other than their brief reminder to act like adults after Nicholas and Will were supposed to pair up during the farmer's market event, they hadn't said anything about the drama in the house either.

"But how far will they let it go? Surely they won't let someone get hurt?"

"The problem may be not seeing the potential for hurt until it's too late to stop it." Nicholas rubbed the back of his neck. "You need to know who you're going to turn to if things go south."

"I suppose if worst comes to worst, I'll speak with Rhonda or Daniel." Livvy sighed. "They're probably the easiest for the contestants to access, and they would also know who to go to with the information." She raised her now tepid mug of cocoa in mock salute. "Here's to Will getting eliminated tomorrow so we don't have to deal with any of this."

Nicholas raised his mug. "I'll drink to that."

"Agreed." Evan drained his mug and set it on the end table beside the sofa. Livvy let him take her now empty cup and place it next to his. "But as much as I want it to work that way, I have a sneaking suspicion it's not going to happen. You and Will are the only contestants who haven't faced an elimination round. I don't see either of you heading home tomorrow. Nicholas and I are another story."

Livvy bristled. "Don't sell yourselves short. You two have been to elimination, but you could look at it like Will and I are due. I won't have either of you giving up."

"Simmer down." Nicholas smiled. "We don't plan on giving up. Neither of us is a quitter."

"We're in this to go all the way, just like you and Will." Evan squeezed her shoulder. "And after tomorrow, three of us will be one step closer."

"And now the conversation has come full circle." Nicholas yawned. "As great as the company is, I think I'm going to head to our room."

Silence settled over her and Evan after Nicholas left. She forced a grin. "I think I should probably go too."

"Please don't go."

"Why?"

"I need to talk to you, and tonight might be my last chance. I know you weren't ready yesterday, and I understand. I hurt you. But, please, don't go. I couldn't stand it if one of us were eliminated tomorrow, and I hadn't at least tried to set things right."

"It's fine, Evan." She forced a small smile. "Everything's great. No need for apologies or whatever this is. We're good."

"No, we're not good." He dragged the hat from his head, dropping it onto the end table next to him. "Far from it. And I do need to apologize, but not the way you think. Please."

Leaning into the corner of the sofa, she faced him. His eyes had darkened to the deep green she'd seen when he was angry, but he wasn't mad. The pain of his regret reached out to her, tugging at her heart.

She couldn't ignore that look. She cleared her throat. "Okay."

"I'm not sure how to start." Evan sucked in a deep breath. "So, I'm going to jump right into it. First, I didn't know our kiss was your first kiss, and I'm sorry that memory is now clouded with all that's come since then. I'm also sorry I left you with the impression that I believed our kiss was a mistake. You are not a mistake, and neither was our kiss. My thinking is what was all messed up.

"I came here to win, and I saw what was going on between us as a potential distraction from that goal. My mom reminded me that while my goal was winning, God's plan for me at this competition might include something I'd never considered."

Livvy picked at the hem of her T-shirt. "What was that?"

"Maybe God brought me here to find you. And it doesn't mean I won't try my hardest to win. I'm in this until the end. I'll always do my best, even if that means eliminating the woman I've already halfway fallen for. Someone I could completely fall in love with, given a chance. Win or lose, I want to know she's waiting for me at the end of this thing. So, I'm asking her, right now, if she'll forgive me for being an idiot and let us start again."

Staring at him, she sucked in a breath, shocked to learn he didn't regret their kiss. It was true. He wanted to be with her as much as she did him. She hadn't misread the situation. And halfway in love with her? That declaration was a complete surprise, but she couldn't argue with the sentiment. Could she forgive him and begin again?

Forgiveness was a given. It was in line with her faith, and it was a choice that would free not only Evan but herself from the trap of guilt and regret his actions tried to create. Starting again was not such an obvious choice. Being sorry now didn't mean Evan wouldn't hurt her again. She'd seen enough to know hurt was inevitable when two imperfect people got together.

This time, she understood his thinking, had shared some of the same thoughts about the competition and their budding romance. What if the next hurt wasn't as relatable? What if it came without warning and made zero sense to her? But what if she never gave him a chance and missed out on the love God would use to make her life experiences richer? Was Evan worth the risk?

"Yes."

"Yes, you'll forgive me?" His brows drew together. "Or yes, we can begin again?"

She smiled and leaned in close. With her face inches from his own, she looked him in the eyes. "Yes. And yes."

Without waiting for his reaction, she closed the distance between them. When he didn't immediately respond to her lips against his, she started to pull away. She sighed as he wrapped her in his arms and pulled her close. His lips were soft and warm, drawing her response without hesitation. His hand traveled from her shoulders and grazed along her neck until his fingers wove through her hair. He deepened the kiss before leaning away, leaving her wanting more.

"I could be wrong." She smirked as she ran her fingers over her lips. "But I don't think many choir boys kiss like that."

His eyes lit up with his laughter as he stood. "Come on. It's time we head to our rooms too."

Only minutes later, nestled under her covers in the dark, Livvy couldn't stop her smile though no one was there to see it. She and Evan were going to be okay. Whether they moved from halfway in love to fully in love or friendship was the end result of this beginning, the awkwardness was gone. The next few days would be amazing.

Or would they? Tomorrow's competition could change everything. Their relationship might survive, but changes were inevitable. There was no escaping it, and the reality weighed on her. She might have played it off when talking with the guys, but she did take Will's actions seriously.

Just thinking of losing the security she had with both Nicholas and Evan in the house made her stomach ache. They hadn't even come to any solid conclusions about the strange happenings in the competition.

"Don't even get me started on how much I need to win this thing." She was glad there were no cameras in the bedrooms. The last thing she needed was to become the crazy contestant who talked to herself in the middle of the night, but she couldn't help it. Too many loose ends had her mind whirring like a washing machine on spin cycle.

Was there going to be drama? Who was causing the problems? Who would no longer be a member of the house after the elimination round? What would happen to her budding romance with Evan if one of them was eliminated? Could she truly win this? Did she want to win if it meant her friends would lose? If she didn't win, what would happen to The Sugar Cube?

Livvy huffed and threw the warmth of her covers aside. She moved to the armchair by the window and looked out at the night sky. It was beautiful and immense, reminding her how small she was compared to the rest of creation.

But the God who made the universe had also made her, loved her, and promised to care about what she was going through. When sleep was elusive, there was only one place she could turn. It should have been the first place, but He would still be there waiting for her.

"Father God, I'm sorry I didn't turn to You immediately after the anxious thoughts began. I know better than relying on myself for answers or peace. You tell us to bring our petitions with thanksgiving and focus our hearts on what is good and right; that You have peace for us that goes beyond the unknown circumstances. I ask Your forgiveness for waiting to come to You.

"You have plans for my life, and You knew all of my days before I took my first breath. No matter what happens or doesn't happen, You aren't surprised. You know the issues we've had on set and in the house. Lord, I want to win. But more than that, I want to be an example of Your love and character to those around me and those who will watch the show. Help me compete with grace and integrity, win or lose.

"And thank You for this opportunity. Thank You for bringing me wonderful friends and allowing me to share my faith with them. Thank You for what I've learned and how I've grown through these challenges. Thank you for the friends who've become family and a chance for a relationship with the best guy I've ever met. For all of this, I thank and praise you. Amen."

Having sought God out in the same way since junior high youth group studied Philippians, Livvy wasn't at all surprised to find her eyes growing heavy by the end of her prayer. The weight of unanswered questions lifted, leaving the lightness of God's peace as she focused on the joys He had already provided for her. She climbed into bed and fell asleep without giving another thought to the possible struggles ahead.

18

Livvy tucked a stray strand of hair back into her mint and white polka-dotted headband before adjusting the tie on her matching apron. She'd always loved that something extra the deep gray trim added to the ensemble. With a full night's peaceful sleep, she found she could appreciate the simple things that added to the day. Not even Will could dampen her mood.

Besides, Parker Kelly was going to be in the studio again. Her creation would be sampled and judged by one of the best bakers around. While it might be what was causing the butterflies to dance in her belly, it was also an amazing once-in-a-lifetime opportunity, and she was grateful for it.

Taylor and Adeline stayed in their seats at the judge's table, letting Parker have the floor from his stance behind his chair. "Lady and gentlemen, I had the honor of hosting you at Frosted yesterday. I saw you in action, trying to recreate my cake, and you did well. However, the cake was still my design and my cake. Today, you're going to change that. Using yesterday's cake as a basic idea to build from, I want you to wow me with a cake that tells me all I need to know about you."

Adeline spoke as Parker took his seat next to her. "You have four hours, and your time begins now."

Livvy wasted no time picking up her basket and running for the pantry. She found her inspiration effortlessly. Fresh blueberries and lemons joined the basic ingredients in her basket before she made her way back to her station. Four hours was more than enough time to complete the ode-to-self she sketched out.

She pulled a glass prep bowl from a shelf under her countertop and grabbed the flour from her basket. Though she could make this recipe in her sleep, Livvy paid careful attention to every scoop and spoonful added to the bowl. There was no room for error as the competition neared the finish line. She wouldn't go home for a failure to measure properly.

With her cakes in the oven, Livvy took a moment to gather her thoughts. She glanced at the other competitors. They looked as focused as she felt. There wasn't a shadow of doubt on any of their faces. Great. She didn't want to win because someone got rattled. That was fine early in the competition, but they were supposed to be top-notch professionals at this point.

Her eyes darted to the countdown clock. Right on schedule. With her space cleared of measuring cups and mixing bowls, Livvy worked color into balls of fondant until the largest one was swirled gray and white, and a smaller one was a light teal. She smiled. This was going to work perfectly.

Without added drama vying for her attention, Livvy stayed in her creative zone until she finished the last detail on her cake.

Will had already plated and stood with his arms crossed. His look oozed the arrogance of a man who knew victory was only moments away. Nicholas and Evan were putting the finishing touches on their creations. Hopefully, they'd all prove Will wrong. It would be nice for the trio of friends to have the house to themselves for the night and to go into the next day's competition with nothing but well-wishes for each other.

"Time!" Taylor's deep voice called a close to the competition.

Will presented first while Livvy waited her turn to carry her creation to the judging table. Evan followed. Parker Kelly must have gotten the memo on keeping a poker face during judging since his facial expression didn't change. How did these people chew without even seeming to move their mouths at all?

As Evan stepped away from center stage, Livvy picked up her offering and moved to take his place. She placed it carefully on the table and stepped back.

"I enjoyed today's task. I try to incorporate elements of my style or taste into every cupcake or specialty cake I make for The Sugar Cube, but to take another baker's creation and meld it with my personality was an added challenge. I kept the gray and white marbled fondant while making the color swirls more subtle.

"While Mr. Kelly may not know this about me, I'm sure Taylor and Adeline have realized my penchant for fifties-style aprons and headbands, most of which are polka-dotted. In honor of this style choice, I've included a teal fondant ruffle with white polka dots made of tiny candy pearls around the base of each layer.

"I carried over the theme into my cupcakes using gray and white polka-dotted cupcake wrappers and topping them with a teal fondant bow complete with a single candy pearl in the center of each one. I also switched out the classic white cake Mr. Kelly used for one more fitting my tastes. Both the cakes and cupcakes are a moist lemon cake with fresh blueberries. The citrus gives the cake a bright, fun flavor, while the blueberries continue the polka dot theme. Enjoy."

Livvy had long ago stopped hoping for a sneak peek into the thoughts of the judges. She patiently waited as they cut into the cake and made sure one of her cupcakes was in front of each judge. As they finished sampling her items, she nodded and moved back to her spot so Nicholas could step in front of the judges.

His cake was beautiful, but all of today's cakes were as artistic. Livvy watched as Nicholas moved away from the table.

The judges leaned toward each other with whispered comments flying between them.

When Adeline and Taylor turned to Mr. Kelly with unmistakable frowns drawing their lips down, a surge of adrenaline shot through Livvy. Mr. Kelly seemed to be gasping for breath as his fingertips rubbed over his lips. Adeline motioned a stagehand over to them, and as quickly as he arrived, he ran from the set.

Within seconds he was back with the on-set EMT. She'd never seen a dose of epinephrine administered before, and she hoped she never would again. It wasn't so much the injection procedure that bothered her as much as the situation itself. Quicker than she would have guessed possible, Mr. Kelly sat back and took a deep breath. The EMT spoke to him, eliciting an answering nod before Mr. Kelly followed him backstage.

A producer came out to Taylor and Adeline. Set jaws evoked a sense of doom. They glanced at Nicholas as they continued their private conversation. His face was pale, and his eyes never left the group at the front of the room. The producer walked away, and Taylor addressed the group.

"While Parker is undergoing additional evaluation, we believe, thanks to the quick response of our EMT, he will recover from this allergic reaction without additional complications. However, there are definitely issues we need to investigate further in regards to what happened. You will go to the response room and wait until we can determine what happened and how it happened. You are dismissed."

He and Adeline didn't wait for them to exit before making their way to the producer waiting off to the side. Rhonda and Daniel entered to usher Livvy and the others into the reaction room. They barely had time to sit on the sofas before Will broke the uneasy silence.

"What did you put in your cake? We all heard the guy is allergic to nuts of any kind. You couldn't possibly have forgotten this soon. Or maybe you didn't pay attention in the first place."

Nicholas's chest heaved. "I didn't put anything in my cake that wasn't supposed to be there." His tone was controlled though his eyes spoke volumes about the disdain he felt for Will. "I heard his warning the same as everyone else, and I wouldn't play with someone's life like that."

One eyebrow raised high. "Really? Then explain to me how Parker Kelly happened to have an allergic reaction immediately after eating your cake."

"I don't know." Nicholas's voice was quiet as he dropped his head into his hands.

"Don't worry." Livvy moved next to him and put her arm around his shoulders. "The producers are going to find out what happened. It's all going to work out. You heard what they said. Mr. Kelly will be fine, and no one," she shot a look at Will, "is going to blame you for this. It's an accident. You weren't malicious or careless."

"We'll see." Will shrugged his shoulders. "There's no telling what the judges will do. I mean, they can't exactly judge without their guest judge. And I'm fairly certain Mr. Kelly won't be inclined to pass you on to the semi-finals after you tried to kill him."

"Will!" The angry tone of Evan's voice caused even Livvy to sit a little straighter.

"Fine. After he had an allergic reaction to something in someone's cake. Whatever words you want to dress it up with, it changes nothing. Nicholas is going to elimination today."

Nicholas groaned. Livvy pulled his hands away from his eyes and held one in her own. "You know as well as we all do that going to the elimination round doesn't have to mean the end of your run on the show. You've come through it before, and you can do it again."

The conversation stalled as everyone became occupied with their thoughts. If only they had an inkling of what was going on outside the reaction room doors. Any little detail could help ease their concerns. Staff members brought them lunch after two hours of waiting and wondering but didn't say a word about what was happening.

Livvy gathered their empty plates and cups to dump them in the trash can in the corner of the room. "If they're going to keep us here all day, they might as well send us back to the mansion. At least then we could get some rest instead of sitting here."

"I think that's the point." Nicholas glanced toward the door. "The strange happenings have finally inflicted enough serious damage to get the producers' attention. They can't exactly have a high-profile guest judge nearly die on the show. It wasn't a top priority before, but it has to be now. And they're convinced one of us is responsible."

"Well, you are the one whose cake nearly did in the guest judge." Will sneered at Nicholas.

"Which is exactly why the culprit couldn't be Nicholas." Livvy rolled her head slightly, trying to relax her shoulders. "He wouldn't sabotage himself. That makes no sense."

"Sabotage or coincidences, Nicholas and I are the only ones in this room who've been impacted by the odd occurrences." Evan looked directly at Will.

He didn't include her in his veiled accusation. With Nicholas unofficially cleared only seconds earlier, Will's guilt in Evan's mind was there for all of them to see. Will's chin lifted. The muscles in his jaw flexed.

Great. All they needed was for a real fight to break out. As if they weren't in enough trouble.

A knock barely preceded Daniel's entry into the room. Oblivious to the tension, he waved them from the room. "Okay gang, they're calling all of you to a meeting in the board room with the judges and producers. Charles Lind, the series showrunner, is running the meeting. Let's go."

Livvy had never been called to the principal's office, but she was sure the long, silent walk to the board room had to feel the same. Did they know who was causing all the problems? Would they be kicked off the show? She glanced at Will. He seemed as unruffled as ever. Strange, if he was the one about to be in the hot seat.

Wait. What if they canceled the show due to all the extenuating circumstances? Win or lose, she counted on the notoriety the show would give her to increase business and make up for the time she was gone.

She sucked in a deep breath. *God is in control. I don't need to worry because God is in control.* Livvy continued to repeat those words until they made it to the board room and found their seats.

A stern-looking man stood at the head of the table. His black suit was perfectly tailored, a ruby red shirt complementing his silvering hair. His heavy-framed glasses were all unyielding right angles, like his posture. Charles Lind, the man leading the meeting. He looked familiar, but she couldn't remember him ever addressing them before. He must have been in the line-up of stuffy men and women introduced as the highest of the higher-ups involved with *Cake That*'s production.

Mr. Lind stared at each of them for a long moment. The silence was oppressive. Livvy wasn't sure anyone in the room continued to breathe, herself included, under the weight of his displeasure. As he opened his mouth to speak, the occupants of the room seemed to inhale in unison.

"*Cake That* has only had one season so far. But don't mistake me for an amateur. I've been the showrunner for several successful reality and competition shows. In all those episodes of all those shows, never have I seen such antics. We wanted to believe these events were not planned. We can no longer take that stance. It is intentional, and it is unprofessional at best.

"Today, we've seen it at its worst, causing harm to Parker Kelly. You are professionals in the food industry. You know the seriousness of food allergies, yet one of you flagrantly placed Mr. Kelly in harm's way. In this case, Mr. Kelly has recovered completely, but that is not the point. Your behavior has escalated in ways that could cause harm or even death. I will not tolerate it."

Livvy jumped as Will's palm smacked the table. "How dare you speak to—"

"You have a lot of nerve raising your voice to me." Mr. Lind pointed a finger at Will. "I can expel you from this show. If you were wise, you'd sit there quietly. One only has to look at the facts of these events to see you top the list of potential culprits."

The man nodded to someone behind Livvy, and Rhonda worked her way around the table. She handed Mr. Lind a clipboard and moved back to her spot without a word.

"It seems on day one you collided with Emma, which resulted in her failure to complete a decent cake." He flipped through the first few pages. "She ended up in elimination and lost. On day two, Genevieve asked you for sugar and retrieved it from where you told her you put it, only to find out later the container was filled with salt instead of sugar. She was going to elimination but chose to walk off set instead."

"She could have competed and stayed."

He held up his hand. "I'm not finished. After this incident, Evan's oven temperature was mysteriously turned up too high, resulting in a trip to elimination. And after a day free from disaster, a flat tire and a changed recipe card sent Nicholas and then Evan to elimination.

"In some way, you were tied to every problem. And you and Livvy, who you have been trying to seduce since she got here, are the only contestants that haven't been targeted. How do you explain that, Will?"

Will's eyes narrowed. "I can't." His voice was quiet but sure. "I can only say I did nothing wrong. I don't need to cheat to beat these people. And as for Livvy, she may have captured my attention for a moment, but I lost interest as soon as I got beyond her looks. She's not the type of person I'd give the time of day."

The man's eyebrow quirked. "Hmm. Well, I guess it doesn't

matter. The fact remains that you two haven't suffered at the hands of our saboteur. And of the two of you, you're the one involved in the circumstances.

"However, I am a fair man. Our people will spend the night reviewing footage for evidence of tampering. If we find any, you will be released from competition immediately." He looked at the production crew scattered around the room. "Rhonda, please pick two cameramen and two producers to work with and go over all the material from the competitions. Make a note of anything questionable."

"Sir, I would like to be on this team," Daniel spoke up beside Rhonda.

"Excuse me? What's your name again?"

"Daniel."

"Thank you for the offer, Dan, but we have this covered. The team I've requested will find the proof we need to take decisive action against the culprit." He punctuated his decree with a pointed look at Will, who stared back without flinching.

Far from cool, Will's lips were pressed thin, and eyes narrowed. He seethed as Mr. Lind dismissed them to return to the mansion for the evening. The silence choked the quartet on the ride. As much as her thoughts followed the same path as Mr. Lind's, she wondered if he hadn't been hasty in practically declaring Will the culprit before gathering the information to prove it.

The idea that it could be nothing more than a witch hunt with Will as the intended target created a sense of pity for him. It would be humiliating for an innocent man. Of course, that was the point. None of them genuinely believed Will could be innocent.

19

W ill didn't speak the entire thirty-minute drive back to the house. As soon as they came through the front door, he stomped his way up the stairs.

Livvy frowned. "Should someone go after him?"

"No. Innocent or not, he's been through the wringer today," Nicholas spoke without taking his eyes from the stairs. "I think it's better we let him work out some of that anger on his own. We wouldn't want him letting loose on anyone else."

"I suppose you're right. I just feel bad for him."

"So, you think he's innocent now?" Evan nudged her shoulder with his.

"I don't know. If he's not, then he's probably sulking because he's about to be caught. But if he is innocent, then being accused like that in front of everyone would be hard to swallow, especially for a man with Will's inflated ego."

Evan's hand grasped hers. His smile was faint, but something glowed in his eyes as he looked at her.

"You're amazing, you know that?"

"Oh, sure, I know. Why did it take you so long to see it?"

"I mean it. After everything he's said to you and how he's

treated you, you can still find it in your heart to feel bad for him. Most people would just claim karma and move on."

"First of all, I don't believe in karma."

"Neither do I. It doesn't mesh well with my faith. I meant it more in general."

"I figured. I do, however, believe our actions have natural consequences, and one day he will have to reap the results of how he has treated people. But if—and that's a big if—Will is innocent in this, he doesn't deserve to reap the consequences of someone else's bad behavior, even if his own is atrocious."

"And if he is guilty?" Nicholas spoke from the doorway to the kitchen.

Livvy glanced up the stairs and back to Nicholas. "Then he can stay in his room and sulk. I won't feel sorry for him at all."

"We can agree on that." Nicholas nodded. "Now, how about dinner? I'll throw some burgers on the grill if you two will get the tomatoes, onions, and lettuce ready. And maybe grab a couple bags of chips from the pantry."

"Sounds like a fair trade to me." Evan clapped Nicholas on the shoulder as he walked past him into the kitchen.

"But only if you let us do the dishes, too. You have the hard part of the meal, after all." Livvy followed the guys into the next room and grabbed a knife from the butcher block before rummaging through the fridge for the needed veggies.

"Deal." Nicholas took the tray of burger patties from the fridge and made his way to the back patio.

After making short work of the vegetable prep, Livvy and Evan went outside to sit at the table while Nicholas finished the burgers. After the eventful day, they were content to eat in peaceful silence. Livvy guessed the same thing was on all of their minds, but they couldn't keep rehashing it. They didn't have the facts, and sitting around guessing at answers wasn't going to help the situation.

"I think I'm going to run a plate up to Will." Nicholas tossed his napkin onto the table and stood. "He may not want it, but at least he'll have the chance to eat if he does. Then I think I'll call it a night and head to our room. But don't worry about being quiet when you come up. I doubt I'll be sleeping."

Evan swallowed his last bite of burger. "You go ahead. Livvy and I will fulfill our part of the bargain and get these dishes cleaned up."

He stopped in the doorway, balancing Will's plate balanced on one hand, and smiled. "Can I say I'm glad to see you two worked out your differences?"

Without waiting for a response, he continued on his way to Will's room. Evan looked at her. His mouth opened like he wanted to say something, but he simply shrugged. Livvy giggled as she stood and gathered empty plates.

"I guess we don't need to make an announcement or anything then. Come on. Let's get things cleaned up."

Working together to load the dishwasher and put away leftovers, it didn't take long for Livvy and Evan to finish. Livvy washed her hands and folded the dish towel onto the counter. She sighed as Evan's arms slid around her, then leaned her head against his shoulder.

He lowered his head next to hers, and his breath tickled a lock of hair against her cheek. She smiled, pushing it behind her ear.

"What's going to happen after tomorrow?" His voice was barely above a whisper.

"I don't know." She lifted her shoulders the tiniest bit. "Maybe they'll find their answers tonight, and tomorrow we'll all know who did it."

"Not about the show." He squeezed her tighter. "I mean, what's going to happen with us? If one of us gets eliminated, or if the show gets canceled because of all the drama, either way, it will be time to go home. I'm not ready for one of us to be in Texas while the other one is in Missouri."

The warmth sparked by his desire to be near her was chilled by the cold reality of his words. Tomorrow could end it all for them. If it didn't, if they both advanced to the semi-finals or even the finals, it meant only three more days together at best. What would happen to them?

"I don't know. What do you want to happen?"

Cool air hit her arms and back as Evan loosened his hold on her. He turned her to face him and brushed a thumb across her cheek. "I want us to have a chance. I want to see where this goes apart from television cameras and all the contrived drama."

"That's what I want, too." She licked her lips. "I've never felt this way about anyone before, but I've never really dated before. All I know is your friendship means too much to me to give it up without a fight." She tilted her head and gave what she hoped was an impish grin. "And I'll admit your kisses are pretty special too."

"My kisses, huh?" His dimples appeared through the scruff on his cheeks. "You mean these kisses?" He brought a hand to the nape of her neck then wove it into her hair. His other hand cupped her cheek as his head dipped to bring his lips to hers.

Her hands slipped around his waist before she slid one up his back to play in the hair peeking out from under his soft hat. Livvy's head swam as she let herself enjoy the feel of his warm, soft lips against hers. Before she was ready, he pulled away.

"Was that right? Was that one of the kisses you think are pretty special?"

She opened her eyes to his cheesy grin. His eyes twinkled.

"You think you're a comedian." She stepped away from him with a playful swat to his bicep. "I have news for you. You're not funny."

"If I'm not funny," he laughed and the sound had her fighting her own case of the giggles. "Why are you trying so hard to keep from laughing?"

"I'm not." She fought to keep a straight face.

"Yes, you are." He took a step closer.

"I am not, and you stay right where you are." She thrust her hands out in front of her and saw the twinkle in his eyes. "That is not a challenge, mister."

"Mister?" He acquiesced and leaned against the nearby counter. "That's not a good title. How about the man of your dreams or love of your life? I think those are more fitting."

She let herself laugh. "My, aren't we full of ourselves this evening? And what makes you think either of those are accurate descriptions of you?"

"Are you saying they're not?" He folded his arms across his chest.

The movement drew her eyes to the black T-shirt pulled tight across perfectly chiseled muscles. She remembered all too well how he looked coming up out of the pool, and it was enough to make her heart falter in its rhythm. He was undeniably attractive, but love was more than that.

She glanced up to find his eyes on her. Her cheeks warmed at having been caught staring, but she didn't want to be misunderstood. "I'm not sure we're at the love of our lives stage quite yet. Let's give ourselves time to grow into that one. But the man of my dreams? Sure. You can be the man of my dreams."

"Good." He smiled like he'd just won the *Cake That* grand prize. "Because you're definitely the only woman in my dreams."

Livvy's smile felt bright enough to light up all of L.A., maybe even the whole state of California. God had brought a man into her life who cherished her and treated her with respect as a woman and a person.

And he wanted a relationship that would outlast their time in the mansion. She had hoped as much when she realized the attraction was mutual, and the uncertainties of their future faded in the light of this new revelation. She and Evan would make it just fine. She was sure of it.

20

The contestants were ushered straight to the same board room they'd been reprimanded in the day before. Taking the same seats, they waited in the empty room for the verdict. They didn't have to wait long.

The entourage of production assistants filed in and took their places against the wall. Rhonda and Daniel were among them. Wearing blank expressions, neither even glanced toward the contestants. Odd, considering they spent more time with the contestants than anyone else. Was it a harbinger of things to come? Livvy hoped not.

Mr. Lind entered the silent room and proceeded straight to the head of the table. Without preamble, he turned to Will. "It seems I owe you an apology. The team I tasked with scouring the footage from the competition returned their findings this morning. Though you were a factor in each disaster, they assured me of your innocence in each and every instance of sabotage."

"Thank you." Will's shoulders relaxed.

Livvy didn't have time to process the humble response before Mr. Lind continued.

"And my team has also confirmed without a doubt the incidents involving salt in the place of sugar, the recipe tampering, the flat tire, the oven fire, and this latest issue with Mr. Kelly's allergic reaction are indeed instances of sabotage."

"But who?" Rhonda's voice broke the tense silence.

"Before we discuss that, there is more pertaining to the show we need to cover." Mr. Lind held up a hand. "As the showrunner, the presence of tampering within the competition leaves me to determine whether or not the show can continue with integrity. To lose our reputation as an honest competition would be a death sentence.

"However, it is clear from the evidence that the sabotage only resulted in competitors being sent to the elimination round. That being the case, each victim had the opportunity to redeem themselves. Therefore, we will not suspend the competition at this time."

Whispered conversations filled the air with a relieved buzz. Livvy joined Will, Evan, and Nicholas in sinking back against their seats. Now that Will was cleared and the competition was safe from cancelation, it felt like a ten-ton weight was lifted from her shoulders. If the others' newly relaxed postures were any indication, the same weight had been lifted from them as well.

Only two questions remained. If Will was innocent of tampering with the competition, who had sabotaged everyone, and why did they do it?

Rhonda started to speak, but Daniel placed a hand on her arm. She glared at him before shaking it off and addressing Mr. Lind.

"I'm thrilled the show will continue. Our bakers have done a fine job this season, especially with the unforeseen events trying to derail their efforts. And though I in no way condone the person's actions, I have to admit the added drama won't hurt ratings. Between that and the romantic tension in the house, we have ratings gold on our hands."

Why did Rhonda have to include the bit about romance in the speech? Livvy felt all eyes on her and wanted to crawl under the table. When Evan slid his hand over hers in a show of solidarity, quiet *oohs* and *ahhs* could be heard from some gathered in the room. Livvy swallowed. Hiding under the table was looking better and better.

While she appreciated Evan's willingness to acknowledge their relationship in public, she wasn't sure she was ready for the spotlight to shine on it quite so glaringly. The frown from the newly-acquitted Will across the table from them didn't help matters.

"But solid ratings or not, we still need to protect the show's integrity." Rhonda smiled sweetly at Livvy before taking a step out of the ranks of crew members to continue her address. "That means taking measures to make sure this doesn't happen again. Do you know who did this?"

Mr. Lind nodded stiffly. "I believe the guilty party left ample evidence on the videos, and the team I put in place to scour those tapes has compiled all the data. However, this individual will be better dealt with in a more intimate group. I would like the head of each production team to stay. This includes the lead camera, makeup, lighting, and sound people. The director will stay, as well as Rhonda and Daniel.

"The rest of you are dismissed. Contestants head to makeup. This won't take long. Taping the ending of yesterday's episode will commence immediately following our meeting."

Daniel shifted from one foot to the other. His gaze wandered from Mr. Lind to those already working their way from the room and back again. Finally, he stepped forward.

"Sir, I do believe it would serve the show better for me to accompany the contestants and make sure all is in order for taping."

"I disagree." Mr. Lind didn't even look up from the papers in his hand. "The contestants are more than familiar with the process and do not need you. I must insist you stay for the meeting."

Already moving out the door on her way to the makeup chair, Livvy couldn't hear if Daniel replied or not. If he were wise, he'd keep his mouth shut and his head down. Mr. Lind didn't seem like the sort to play around. He was the king of the *Cake That* kingdom, and, historically speaking, arguing with royalty didn't end well.

Outside the makeup room, Rhonda met them. Her face was flushed, and her lips were pinched. Could she have been in the line of fire in the board room? There were no tear tracks on her cheeks, no reddened eyes under her perfect mascara. It couldn't have been too bad for her, but Livvy was sure she was upset.

"I've been sent to fill you in before you continue to today's taping."

The chill in her voice could be felt throughout the room. Rhonda wasn't upset. She was furious. But why?

"It seems the saboteur has been found. I sat there, watched the tapes, and saw it with my own eyes. The snake couldn't have denied if he wanted to, which he didn't. No. He sat there and made excuses. Said we didn't respect him. We didn't take his contributions seriously, even though there would've been no show without him. We put him in a position where he had to prove himself by, and I quote, 'taking whatever steps necessary to ensure healthy ratings for this season.'"

It couldn't be.

"I worked with Dan day in and day out. I worked with him more closely than anyone else on production. I was there to mentor and guide him, and this is how he repays me?"

Livvy's eyes slid shut. Daniel. What would Harper say when she found out? It would break her heart. It didn't matter that everything else Rhonda said was a delusion. It didn't matter that everything he had said about lacking respect and not being taken seriously were true. Why turn to sabotage?

"How would ratings prove anything about Daniel's capabilities? And if he was trying to trip everyone up, why didn't he resort to tricks every day of the competition? We know one day went without incidents of any kind." Will's questions made Livvy's eyes snap open. Yes, she had wondered the same.

"Your second question is easier to answer. In justifying his sabotage, he admitted he only stepped in if the competition didn't seem to offer enough tension on its own. The day in question, you proved you were far less skilled in darts than in baking. He didn't think stepping in was necessary after one of you nearly took out some of the crew members."

"But he's an intern. What was he trying to prove through getting the show better ratings?" Livvy didn't see how it would help Daniel for the show to do well.

"He says he came up with the idea for *Cake That*." Rhonda threw her hands in the air with her fingers fanned wide. "But you couldn't prove it by me. He thought if the show took off, he'd be able to gain producer status instead of being an intern and working his way up the ladder like everyone else. Ridiculous, really."

Livvy had heard the same story from Harper. "So, it isn't true? Daniel didn't come up with the idea?"

A dramatic eye roll and shake of her head added to Rhonda's sense of theatrics. "How would I know? That was a closed-door meeting I wasn't party to. What I do know is Daniel worked on Charles' previous production with him as an intern. Is it possible? Sure. Do the facts matter in Hollywood? Probably not as much as people think."

One of the production assistants stuck her head out a door down the hall. "We're about ready in there, Rhonda. Are the competitors ready?"

"We'll be there in a minute." Rhonda waved her on. "They're just about ready." She turned her attention back to the group. "Anyway, that's enough talk of Daniel's betrayal. Luckily, we still have a show to tape. Yesterday's episode will be wrapped up today, no matter what. They decided to judge based on the cakes you presented yesterday." She looked at Nicholas.

"Of course, this will be on taste and presentation alone. Mr. Kelly's unfortunate allergic reaction won't factor into the decision at all. Now, let's go find our places, everyone."

The group hustled down the hall and into place in front of the judges' table. Taylor and Adeline were already present. The empty chair on the other side of Adeline couldn't be ignored. It was a glaring reminder of everything they'd dealt with throughout the competition, especially the last two days. Would they even address the issue on air?

Taylor cleared his throat. All eyes moved to him. "Thank you for your patience as we got Mr. Kelly the help he needed. He is doing well, though he cannot join us for the remainder of this competition as we'd hoped. Our thoughts are with him as he recovers."

"It seems almond flour was improperly labeled in our pantry." Adeline's hands came together in front of her. "That error and the one who was responsible for it have been dealt with, and the resulting reaction will not be held against Nicholas. Today's judging was on taste and presentation alone."

Taylor nodded his agreement. "Now for the results. One cake stood out from the rest as the confectionary embodiment of its creator. Bright, full of surprise, and just a little bit quirky, this cake was as much a pleasure to eat as it was to look at. Livvy, you are an artist with cake. Take your spot in the viewing area."

An excited squeal escaped before she could stop it. For the second time in the competition, her cake was singled out as the one to beat. And Taylor called her an artist. There wasn't a better compliment than that, especially after Parker Kelly's positive praise only two days earlier.

"Nicholas, while we aren't counting the use of almond flour against you, your cake fell short in displaying who you are as a baker and a person." Adeline summed up the results. "It tasted great, but it didn't leave us with a clear image of you. Evan, your cake was a perfect representation of who you are, but the cake itself was a little dry.

"The same could be said about your cake, Will. Your design evoked everything we've come to expect from you. Bold colors and design exuded the confidence you've shown in every event this season. However, your cake was not executed as proficiently. The flavors seemed to fight for center stage, and the cake was not as moist as some of the others you've given us."

Taylor looked at each individual before landing on one. "Evan, please join Livvy in the viewing section. Will and Nicholas prepare to face off in the elimination round."

Evan's relief was almost tangible. His smile as he took a seat next to her was bright. The only time she'd seen it brighter was when he looked at her. She touched her hand to his in congratulations, removing it before it could become a focal point for one of the many cameras scattered over the set. Evan was safe. Nicholas and Will were going head-to-head.

Both were strong competitors. Will was hungry for success. After being erroneously blamed for the show's sabotage, he might even feel he had something to prove. His ego would not suffer defeat well under any circumstances, but even less so with the events of the last few days.

But Nicholas could take him. She was sure of it. Nicholas was a great baker and an amazing designer. Would it be enough to outbake Will and stay in the competition? Livvy could only hope so.

21

"I'm certainly glad all that sabotage nonsense is over. When I beat you two and win the hundred grand, I don't want there to be any question about whether or not I earned it fair and square."

Livvy bit the inside of her cheek to keep from answering back. It only encouraged him to have someone respond. What more could he say if they refused to react? Besides, as much as it pained her to say goodbye to Nicholas, Will won the elimination round free from interference of any kind. She and Evan would have to spend one more night with him, and now that Daniel was removed from the show, she wanted to avoid even a hint of drama in their time together.

She leaned back against Evan, and he put his arm over her shoulders on the back of the loveseat. The gagging sound Will made reminded her of the boys she knew in junior high after the girls in class turned them down. They couldn't handle rejection, either. It had taken her a long time to realize behind their bravado were heavy doses of self-doubt. She glanced at Will.

The twist of his lips broadcast his disgust at their innocent display. There was no way he suffered from the same pre-teen issues of self-worth. He just hated to lose. She was sure of it.

When his juvenile actions didn't garner attention, he returned to his previous topic of conversation. "The question is, which one of you will I be going against in the final episode? Evan's good. But is he good enough to beat you, Livvy? I'm not so sure. You have an off-beat, passionate style about you. And while I'm not a fan, the judges seem to eat it up. No pun intended. I think you'll be the one beside me when I win."

"I wouldn't be too sure of a guaranteed win."

Livvy's stomach clenched as Evan engaged Will in his conversation.

"If I'm remembering correctly, there is only one baker left who has never participated in the elimination round. And it isn't you. It doesn't hurt that her cakes have been singled out as the best of the day multiple times, either. Her off-beat, passionate style, as you put it, might just come out on top."

"I highly doubt that." Will's chin rose. "Livvy and her little polka-dotted aprons are cute, like a gimmick. When it comes to the final round, I'm sure the judges will opt for sophistication and expertise. Providing, of course, that Livvy is even in the final round. I mean, I don't see why she wouldn't be, but you never know, do you?"

"Nope." Evan's jaw clenched but his voice was calm. "You never know what's going to happen."

The conversation stalled, leaving an uneasy silence in its wake. Livvy did her best to ignore Will's glances and pretend everything was as normal as could be. It wouldn't do to let him think he'd made them uncomfortable, and she was done talking about the what-ifs. He shifted in the recliner, continued to watch them, and shifted some more. Finally, he stood.

"As fun as it is sitting here with you two acting all lovey-dovey, I think I'll call it a night."

"Good night." Livvy smiled innocently. "See you tomorrow."

After his footsteps faded, Evan exhaled a deep breath. "I thought he'd never leave. And as much as I didn't want to talk to him about the competition and what might happen tomorrow, I do want to talk to you about it."

Livvy moved from him to the far arm of the loveseat. She pulled a leg up under her as she pivoted to face him. "I can't say I'm looking forward to it, but I know we need to. I'm not sure where to start, though."

When Evan reached across to still her hands, Livvy realized she was wringing them. She looked into his eyes and saw her feelings mirrored. Knowing he understood and might even be feeling the same way, her heart melted a little more.

Could she love someone after such a short time? It seemed impossible, but she didn't have any experience to go on. And while she guessed it was unusual, so were all the circumstances around their relationship. She wanted the best for him and would do anything in her power to see that he had it.

He made her feel like no one ever had. And it wasn't just his kisses or the gentle way he held her hands. He knew her and understood what went on inside her head and heart. Livvy felt she knew him just as deeply. Did all of that add up to love?

When he reached up and tucked a stray strand of hair behind her ear, she couldn't deny the butterflies set into motion. She was mature enough to know thrilling at his touch didn't mean love was present, but woman enough to appreciate it anyway. His eyes darkened with concern as he continued to watch her.

"How are you doing with Nicholas's elimination?"

How could one small question bring stinging tears to her eyes? She blinked them back and shrugged. "I hate it. Nicholas was a friend but also more like family. Being here without him, even if it's only one night, doesn't seem right."

"I don't know if it helps, but sharing a room, Nicholas and I talked a lot." He sat back against the corner of his seat, facing her as she did him. "He thought of you the same way. It's going to be awfully quiet in the room tonight with him gone."

"I feel conflicted. I'm so grateful for the opportunity God's given me through the show. I've made some great friends that I hope to keep after things wrap up here. Harper and Nicholas ..."

"And me?"

She giggled at his pitiful voice and puppy dog eyes. "I wasn't going to list you in the friends' category, but if that's where you want to be, I can oblige." She teased.

Playfulness fled, replaced with a deep huskiness that poured over her like chocolate on a sundae. "What category would you put me in?"

Mercy. She'd opened up a can of worms without even trying. She licked her lips. His gaze dropped to them, but he remained motionless as he raised his eyes to search her face for answers. Her reply came to her immediately.

Could she be so bold? She'd done it before. She leaned toward him until their lips were inches apart and looked him in the eyes.

"This is the category I put you in." She kissed him, relieved when he didn't pull back at her forwardness.

Relief was replaced by excitement as his arms came around her, pulling her closer. She groaned as his arms tightened and the kiss intensified. The realization that they were alone but never really alone recalled her to her senses, and she pulled back just enough to break the spell.

She pressed her lips close to his ear, bypassing his lips with their cute pout of confusion. But she had a message for him alone. "While I'd love to make certain you know where you fit in my life, I've remembered we're not alone. I'd rather not let everyone in America in on the secret."

"I agree." He angled his head so his mouth was next to her ear. "Illusions of privacy aside, it's a good idea anyway. You are much too tempting, and I don't want to cross any lines."

That's when she knew. She'd found a man she wanted to give her heart to, and he'd shown himself worthy of it. She gave him a peck on the cheek as she returned to her side of the loveseat. "Thank you. That means a lot."

"Did I do a good job?"

She didn't need a mirror to know a blush immediately colored her cheeks. "What?" Why did her voice suddenly rebel, making her sound like a breathless Minnie Mouse?

He laughed. "I mean, did I adequately distract you from missing Nicholas?"

"Oh. That. Yes." Livvy covered her face with her hands.

"You do my heart good, Olivia Rae Miller." His laughter continued. "Never in a million years would I have guessed God would bring me to a show like this so I could fall in love."

Livvy froze, staring at Evan with eyes that felt as big as moons. Did he realize what he said? Did he mean it like that, or was it a figure of speech? If he meant it, was he waiting for her to say it back? Her eyes slid shut as he cupped her chin with his hand and caressed her cheek with his thumb. His touch was gentle, and Livvy had never felt more cared for or wanted.

All the questions rumbling through her mind fled as a feeling of contentment settled over her. She sighed, opened her eyes to find him regarding her carefully.

Without taking his eyes from hers, he leaned in as if to share a secret. "Yes, I know what I said. And yes, I meant every word. I love you, Livvy, and no matter what happens tomorrow, I don't want what we have to end."

"I don't either. We just got started."

"Good." He sat back, pulled the green beanie from his head, and gently pushed it down over her wavy hair. His fingers fell from the hat to play with the teal lock of hair cascading to her shoulders from under the knit cap.

"What's this for?" She touched the hat self-consciously. Headbands were fine, but what did she look like in his beanie?

"To show you're my girl, of course." His lips twisted to the side.

"But it's your Gram's hat. I couldn't." She reached to pull it from her hair, but Evan took her hand in his, stopping her.

"Yes, you can."

She shook her head. "Evan, I understand what this beanie means to you, maybe even more than you do at the moment. I know what we've got is special. I can feel it."

"I can, too."

"That's great, but having this amazing thing between us doesn't mean you should give up the one thing that ties you to your Gram. It keeps your connection to her real, tangible, when she's not there."

He smiled softly. "That's exactly why I want you to have it. Even without the beanie, Gram is everywhere around me when I'm at home. Family pictures. Stories we share around the dinner table. In everything I bake."

"But it's ..."

"It's going home with you. When I leave here, I'll have Gram with me. But I won't have you."

"Oh, Evan."

"Take it. That way, I know when you go home, you're taking me with you."

Livvy sniffed as she tugged the hat further onto her head. "Thank you."

Evan pulled her back to rest against his shoulder and softly stroked her arm. She sighed. She couldn't remember receiving a more meaningful gift. But ...

"Evan?"

"Yeah?"

"I've got a purple polka-dotted headband in my room if you want to take part of me with you."

Livvy smiled as his laughter filled the room, easing the weight of emotion.

"I'll take it, and you'll never get it back."

She sat up and turned to face him. "You'll wear my headband?"

One finger lifted in the air. "Correction. I said I'd take it with me. In fact, I'll keep it with me all the time. I never said I'd wear it."

His lips were soft and warm, and their touch was gone almost as soon as they met hers, leaving a cool tingle where they'd been.

"But you?" The husky quality of his voice turned her insides to jelly. "You might consider trading in your headbands for the beanie because I've never seen you look more adorable than you do right now."

Pleasure at his compliment must be written all over her face. Evan thought she was adorable in his hat. If it meant he always looked at her like he was now, she just might take his advice.

22

Livvy swallowed the last gulp of her extra caffeinated hot tea and threw the cup into the trash bin before stepping onto the *Cake That* set. She wouldn't lose the competition just because she and Evan decided to stay up too late discussing what they would do if one of them got eliminated in the day's event.

But even without the added boost of caffeine, Livvy had to admit she felt pretty good. Must be a side effect of being in love with the right guy.

Adjusting her headband, she stepped into place in front of the judges' table. The morning started with Evan's beanie sitting next to her headband on the dresser. For a moment, she'd even put it on, but her nerve fled before she left her bedroom.

Normal levels of attention she could handle without a problem, but even her boundaries were not prepared for the scrutiny that would come with donning Evan's signature look. Distraction had no place in her semi-final event. She had to bring her best to whatever the judges threw at them.

"Competition this season was strong, but you three had what it takes to rise to the top." Adeline greeted the group. "You have reason to be proud of the cakes you've created, but now isn't the time to celebrate. One of you is standing in this kitchen for the last time. You'll have to use every ounce of creativity and skill you've acquired to avoid that fate."

"Today's challenge is all about change." Taylor picked up the speech waving his upturned hand at four small white boxes at the front of the table. "Ladies first, Livvy. Please choose a box."

Livvy carefully considered the choices before taking the first box. Using her thumb and forefinger, she pulled out the most delicate crystal snowflake she'd ever seen.

Taylor continued. "As you might guess from Livvy's selection, the change we want to showcase is the changing of the seasons. Inside each container is an item representing one of the four seasons. Each of you is tasked with making a cake and cupcake duo that captures the essence of your seasons. Livvy's, of course, is winter. Evan, you're next."

Evan, then Will, examined the identical boxes carefully, though they knew as well as Livvy, it gave them no advantage. No hint could be gleaned as to the contents which would make all the difference in the competition.

With only one box remaining unclaimed, Evan removed a ceramic Easter egg from his. Will emptied the contents of his into his hand, revealing a tiny wooden pumpkin.

Winter, Spring, and Autumn each had distinct flavor profiles, color schemes, and major holidays associated with them. The level playing field would keep them on their toes and the competition tight. Livvy had to keep her focus for this one.

"You have four hours, and your time starts now."

A plan topped her list of needs as Livvy raced to her workstation. The pantry and its abundance of ingredients could wait. She couldn't afford to work haphazardly. Each part, from flavors to design, had to work together. Her cakes had to be perfect. It took only minutes for the sketchpad to progress from general ideas to a harmonious blending of every element. She grabbed her basket and headed to the pantry.

With all she needed to bring her sketch to life, Livvy set ingredients out on her station and paused long enough to take a calming breath. Finishing in time was necessary, but sloppy work would not impress the judges. She closed her eyes and took another deep breath, silently prayed for God's help to do her best and to take pride in the outcome—no matter what. Only then did she reach for the first ingredients.

Livvy was familiar with the batter she needed to prepare. As she slid the cakes into the oven, she glanced at the clock. She'd made good use of the time. Now, she could focus on the decorations while they baked. She could do this. She'd finish and present cakes equally delicious and beautiful. Determined to give the judges everything they asked for, she moved on to the fondant. After far too many wasted minutes, she wondered if her goal would be possible.

"Come on. Why won't you work?" Livvy growled, slapping her hand down on the counter. She tossed the fondant in the trash. The fondant for her Parker Kelly cake had worked perfectly. Why couldn't she get this one to have the subtle swirl she wanted?

Time for plan B. Her cakes were almost ready to pull from the oven. Her snowflakes were drying. She had one batch of buttercream ready to go, but without the fondant to cover the cake, it wouldn't be enough. Livvy pulled the mixing bowl from the stand mixer and set it aside. Grabbing a clean one from under the counter, she secured it in place and began measuring ingredients. This had to work. She didn't have time for anything else.

With the final layer of cake covered in rich buttercream, Livvy took a moment to survey her frosting work. Fondant generally provided the ultra-smooth base for decorating, but she had learned long ago attention to detail and patience went a long way in making buttercream work up just as beautifully. Each layer of her cake was smoothed to perfection, a canvas ready to make into a masterpiece. It was time for the snowflakes.

Livvy swiped the back of her forearm across her forehead. She glanced at the countdown clock. Thirty seconds. Not much time to place the delicate snowflake centerpiece in the exact right position. Her hand trembled as she reached toward the top layer. She forced herself to pause, close her eyes, and take a deep breath. She opened them—time to try again. Only seconds remained. If she didn't get the snowflake set this try, the elimination round waited for her.

One more deep breath to still the tremor in her hand before raising the last snowflake to the top of the cake. Easy. Easy. Her hand freed the snowflake and dropped away from her finished creation as Taylor called time.

Adeline folded her hands in front of her. "Livvy, please present your cakes."

She picked them up, carefully walked them to the judges' table, and then stepped back into place. "As you can tell, my theme today is winter. Growing up in the Midwest, we had many cold winter nights, which I have recreated for you. The white bottom layer of my cake represents the snow-covered ground. As you work up the cake, the color transitions from snowy white to the palest of blues to a deep, midnight blue representing a winter night's sky.

"The delicate snowflakes swirling around the cake are made of royal icing, and some are dusted with edible glitter to capture the sparkle of snow under the moonlight. From the time I was little, my favorite way to enjoy those cold winter nights was with a mug of hot chocolate and a peppermint stick to stir it and add a hint of mint to the flavor.

"My cake today pays homage to those favorite flavors. The cake is dark chocolate, and the filling and frosting are peppermint buttercream. I hope you enjoy."

Though she had no idea what they tasted like, Evan and Will's cakes were beautiful. Will's autumn cake evoked a sense of falling leaves and harvest with accents of rich reds, golds, and oranges over dark chocolate frosting. Evan's was as delicately colored in pastels as Will's was dark. The lightest, barely-there blue frosting was trimmed in white with colorful butterflies and flowers expertly arranged around its layers.

Evan and Will flanked her as they stood waiting for their judgment. Competition or not, friends or not, they'd made it this far together. Livvy looked at Will and reached out her hand. His brows lifted in surprise before he clasped her hand. She slipped her other hand into Evan's. He squeezed it and rubbed his thumb along the edge of her finger.

"Congratulations." Taylor clapped his hands. "You three have come a long way since the first day of competition. You've experienced ups and downs and surprises. You've shown yourselves to be not only professionals but experts in your field. You have reason to be proud as the final three.

"Seven other competitors did not fare as well. Today, after the elimination round, another will join the ranks of the eliminated. Only one of you is safe from elimination. But which one?"

Adeline smiled her camera-ready smile. "Judging wasn't easy today. You each did an amazing job transforming your cakes into an expression of your season. The artistry of your creations was spot-on. The cakes themselves were moist and flavorful. With so little we could find wrong, today's judging is less about who lost and more about who stood out a fraction of an inch more than the others. That baker will be safe from elimination while the other two compete to stay."

Their attention swung back to Taylor as he spoke again. "Livvy, you are safe from elimination. Please take a seat in the viewing area."

Livvy dropped the hands she held and covered her mouth in surprise. She was safe. No matter how close the judgment, she won this round. She moved to the viewing area as the judges gave Evan and Will their new orders to make a cake to represent the only season left. Livvy didn't envy them.

Making a cake that embodied summer wouldn't be an easy task. There were almost too many directions one could go, and the only major holiday was Independence Day. She doubted the judges wanted cakes decorated with stars, stripes, and fireworks.

Evan and Will flew into action and kept a steady pace for the next four hours. Other than answering the occasional question from the judges, neither spoke during the two hundred and forty minutes.

Of course, they wouldn't. Of all the competitors, Will and Evan were the least likely to get friendly with each other. Would it have been different if she'd simply rebuffed Will's attempts at getting together and ignored Evan's as well?

It was possible, but she wouldn't feel guilty about her choice. It was the right one, whether Will agreed or not. She couldn't help it that he wasn't mature enough to handle rejection. It would be interesting to see what happened if he had to deal with rejection from the judges as well.

23

Livvy stared out the car window. Other cars flew by in a blur along with the scenery, but she didn't care. Sightseeing was the last thing on her mind. She wanted to get to the house, change into her pajamas, and crawl under the covers for the night.

She tried to swallow the lump in her throat, but it remained. It didn't matter. Even if she did manage to get rid of it, she'd be choked up again in minutes. The feeling had yet to go away permanently.

"I can't be sorry, you know." Will's voice was quiet but still broke through her self-imposed silence. "Evan was a strong competitor. I was just better."

His ego usually made her bristle, but there was something different in his tone this time. It was more humble than his words sounded. Probably the best she could hope for from him. Even this was a major change from his usual behavior.

"I know." She gave a half-hearted smile. "Someone had to go, and this time it was Evan. You won that round fair and square. You've got no reason to feel sorry about that."

"Good." He perked up a little. "I hoped you would be a

bigger person than to hold a grudge against me just because I got your boyfriend kicked off the show."

"Not at all." She shook her head. "I guess I'm just ready for all of this to be over."

"Over? Why look forward to it being over? We've got one last night in an amazing house. Why don't we make it the best night possible? We can order in some Thai, enjoy the swimming pool or hot tub one more time, and maybe even catch a movie on the big screen in the rec room."

None of those were on her list of things to do. But he had a point. It was their last night, and maybe she shouldn't sequester herself in her room all night. "How about Thai food and a movie? No pool. No hot tub."

"Afraid I won't be able to control myself with you in a swimsuit and no lover boy to stand in the way?"

She glared at him. He had ruined it within minutes. He started off like a normal human being, then lost it again, like someone had flipped on the jerk switch without warning. Maybe she should go to her room and stay there all night.

"All right. I'm sorry." He chuckled nervously and gave her an uncomfortable smile. "It was a joke, and it was over the line. We'll do Thai and a movie just like you said."

"And you'll keep your comments to yourself?"

"Yes, I'll keep my comments to myself." He exhaled. "But when you realize you're having a better time with me than you did with anyone else, remember that you asked for my silence. I'll have no choice but to be nice and ignore the signs."

Again, she knew it was probably the best she could expect from him. And it wasn't totally over the line. But she better set him straight anyway. "Deal. But just so we're clear, there won't be any signs given. You might as well forget looking for them."

"Deal."

He extended his hand. She considered it for a moment before shaking. Food and a movie with Will weren't what she expected and nothing she thought she'd ever agree to. But if he could rein in his tendencies to insult and insinuate, the evening might not be a total waste. She might even enjoy it.

In the time it took them to get to the house, order and receive their food, and change into comfortable clothes, the dread hanging over Livvy began to evaporate. By the time the movie was half over, she was actually having fun.

"Really?" Will's voice was as animated as it had been throughout the rom-com. "I'm with the girl. I get the cutesy, bring-them-together aspect of the whole situation—the difference between hugging and leaning and all that. But seriously, who writes this stuff? No one leans. There is no leaning. No man goes around leaning to get a girl's attention."

Livvy covered her mouth as she laughed. Will let her choose one of her favorite chick flicks for the evening without argument and then proceeded to add commentary to every scene, including why she fell for the guy with the bushy eyebrows and how the super's son was cliché. Livvy was surprised by his dry humor and found herself giggling, if not all-out laughing, through most of the movie.

When the final credits rolled, he was still hamming it up as Livvy reached for the empty popcorn bowl and takeout containers. She tensed when his hand grasped her wrist, but he was looking at the dishes.

"Let me take those. I know you were tired when we left the studio. I'll clean up."

"I'll help." She fought back the twinge of guilt at jumping to conclusions. Her smile came easily and honestly as she shook her head. "It's true; I was tired. I've watched all my friends get eliminated from the show. I know it's how it's supposed to be, but it made it hard to come back for one more night. You've made it easier. Thank you."

He opened his mouth but closed it with a shrug, then gathered empty containers while she picked up their cups and the popcorn bowl. What had he been about to say? But then again, maybe she didn't want to know. Maybe he had just successfully stopped the old Will from returning. If so, they'd certainly made some progress through the evening. She followed him into the kitchen and loaded the dishwasher.

"Don't take this as a sign or anything, but you've been different tonight. I kind of wish this Will had shown up for the rest of the show."

He threw the trash in the bin before turning to lean against the counter, his arms folded across his chest. "I'm the same Will I've always been."

"Possibly, but if that's true, you sure did a good job of hiding it. You came across like you thought you were better than everyone at everything, like we weren't worth your time. And I realize that sounds horrible, and I'm sorry. I don't mean to offend or anything. But I've had a great time hanging out with you tonight."

"I don't know." He shrugged. "I've always thought you were worth my time."

She tilted her head and pursed her lips. Why would he choose now to start with the pick-up lines?

"I don't mean it like that. I mean, I did mean it that way in the beginning. I know you're with Evan, and though I definitely do not understand your choice, I won't mess with that. You're the only one of the group I would have picked to go into the finals with me, and not just because you're the most attractive, even though you are. You had my attention from the first challenge because you're a talented baker, more so than anyone else here besides me."

"Then why all the smart remarks about me learning from you?"

"You had my attention right away, but I didn't have yours. The jolly green giant caught your eye from the moment you both stepped into the room that first night. You would've gone for me if he hadn't been here. I had to up my game. I know how it works; I'm the next-to-youngest of five boys. You have to be the best to be worth anyone's time. But even being the best won't do you any good unless you let everyone know you're the best."

She chose to ignore the insulting nickname or correct the misconception that he ever stood a chance with her. He still had a more than healthy ego, but maybe he had his reasons. Everyone wanted to be noticed.

"Being an only child, I can't speak from experience where siblings are concerned. But maybe you shouldn't try so hard."

His skeptical look encouraged her to explain.

"We've had a good time tonight. I'll be honest, I've had more fun with you in this one evening than I have the entire rest of the show. Tonight, you're just you. You haven't tried to impress anyone. You haven't challenged or put anyone down. And I like this Will. Maybe you shouldn't try so hard to prove you're the best at everything and be content to just be Will. And I don't mean to imply I've been perfect. We've all got weaknesses to wrestle with when our strengths get out of control. You've seen the worst of my temper, and I'm sorry for that. I should have said it sooner. Can you forgive me?"

He frowned, rubbing his hand across the back of his neck. Had she said too much? She didn't want to hurt him, but this was the first time she'd seen a side of him that wasn't so alienating.

If the others had seen it too, Will might not have ended up so easy to blame when things went south during the competition. If arrogance was his youthful survival tactic, maybe there was still hope that he would outgrow it. She decided to give him space for his thoughts. She'd pushed him enough with her observations, she wouldn't try to force his forgiveness.

"Well, I guess I'll head up to bed. Tomorrow's a big day. Thanks again for watching the movie with me tonight. It was fun."

"Yeah, it was." Will nodded. "In fact, when I beat you tomorrow, there may even be a tiny part of me that feels bad about it."

"Good night." Livvy walked away, shaking her head. There was the Will she'd known and less than loved.

"Hey, Livvy." His voice stopped her on the stairs, but she didn't turn around. "About the other thing. It's all good. Have a good night."

Livvy smiled and continued to her room. Maybe, hopefully, tonight's fun Will was here to stay.

24

Everyone on set seemed to radiate new levels of energy as Livvy and Will stepped in front of the judges' table. She'd blame it on her nervousness, but maybe it had more to do with the final day of competition and the completion of the show's second season. Perhaps it was a little bit of everything wrapped up together.

Whatever it was, Livvy couldn't stop fidgeting. She smoothed her hand over the hunter-green beanie, secured artfully over her curls, and tugged at her polka-dot apron. It was a lighter, girlier green, but the way the colors complemented each other set loose a few butterflies in her stomach. Evan wasn't here today, but they were still together.

Though she only carried her mom, Evan, and his Gram with her in the tokens she wore, Livvy considered it a privilege to honor their place in her baking journey. Well, she would try to do justice to them all, but she had never worn a cap like this before and wasn't used to the feel of it on her head. Was today the wrong day to try it out? It seemed like a great way to honor those who were previously eliminated.

Would it be more of a distraction? She really didn't need distractions, but it was too late to change. Adeline and Taylor were taking their seats. A crew member wheeled a large screen television next to the table before returning to his place off set.

Adeline clasped her hands together. Livvy would miss that little quirk. Maybe she could get Tabitha to start folding her hands like that before she talked. Livvy bit her lip to hold back a giggle at the thought. It wouldn't do to have the judge think she was being laughed at.

"Will and Livvy, you've made it to the final day. You can take pride in the performances that have brought you here. It's been a great journey for both of you. Let's take a look at some of the highlights."

As she motioned to the screen, it lit up with images of Will and Livvy from earlier days. Clips from the reaction room were spliced together with pictures of their finished cakes, scenes of their hurried baking in the kitchen, and even a few shots from the house. Livvy didn't doubt the video would be enhanced with the proper mood music for the audience at home and leave them feeling nostalgic about the whole season. It was a sweet trip down memory lane for her as well.

The screen went dark, and Taylor addressed them. "Your journey to the finals wasn't a solo trip. You started with eight other competitors. Some you got to know better than others. Let's take a look at those who joined the journey with you."

The screen lit up again. This time images of everyone else played across the screen. They progressed in order from Emma on day one to Evan's elimination just the day before. Seeing Evan, Nicholas, and Harper in their highs and lows caused Livvy's throat to tighten. She discreetly raised her hand to wipe a tear from the corner of her eye and then moved it to touch her beanie as if straightening it.

As the screen darkened again, Adeline waved her hand in Livvy's direction. "I noticed you opted in favor of a beanie today in place of your trademark headband. While I miss the little taste of personality your fashion choices have brought to our competition, it is fitting that you pay tribute to the competitors who have already been eliminated."

"They were part of your journey, and today that journey is going to take center stage." Taylor stepped in. "Your task today is to create cakes that showcase your time on *Cake That*. You'll have to use every decorating trick in your toolbox to wow us with a cake that will not only tell us who you are but who you've become in the course of this competition.

"Your finished cake should leave us without any doubts about how you view your time on the show. You have four and a half hours to complete today's assignment. Your time starts now."

Livvy raced to her workstation and pulled out her notepad. The montage of their time on the show sparked an idea. She needed only a few moments to sketch it out on paper before heading to the pantry. Will was already there, filling his basket.

"Good luck today, Will."

"Thanks, but I don't need luck to win this one."

Same old Will. She sighed. "That's good, because I don't really buy into the idea of luck anyway, but it's the only way I had to say I hope you do well today."

"Thanks." He paused with his hand on a container of flour and glanced in her direction. "And good luck to you, too."

She smiled and nodded. Maybe the new-and-improved Will hadn't disappeared entirely. Given time, he might turn around completely.

But time was not on their side at the moment. Livvy finished filling her basket and returned to her workspace. She had just under four and a half hours to craft a masterpiece and win one hundred thousand dollars. She needed the money as much as Will seemed to need the accolades of winning. Then again, maybe neither of them needed their prize as much as they thought. God would take care of her. He always did.

Winning would be awesome, but after last night, she couldn't feel it would be so horrible for Will to win, either. Well, maybe she wouldn't be devastated to lose, but it was in her nature to try to win. And she could win; it wasn't an impossible dream anymore. Her cakes had been named the best cakes of the day multiple times. One more time wasn't out of reach.

Livvy and Will bantered back and forth, good-natured ribbing that had come a long way from earlier competitions. Time ticked down without mercy, driving them on. Even without sabotage and mishaps, the final episode would be full of intensity. It wasn't quite the turmoil they'd experienced before, but it would still draw in the viewers.

Not that she was complaining about a lack of drama. The pressure to get her cakes done perfectly was high. She wiped her forehead with the back of her hand. How did Evan work in a beanie every day? The added material was making her hotter than normal, and it was warm enough already with the lights, ovens, and constant activity. She unpinned it from her head, revealing the headband that matched her green polka-dotted apron, and tucked it carefully into an oversized pocket.

"There's the Livvy I've been waiting for. It's about time you took off that thing."

"I didn't do it for you." She shook her head at Will's teasing. "I did it because it was making me too hot."

"Baby, you didn't need that ridiculous hat to tell you that. You're always too hot."

She rolled her eyes. Will gave her a sly wink.

Realizing he was simply hamming it up for the show dissipated her slight irritation. "Why don't you give it up and focus on your cakes? You might stand a chance of winning *that* competition."

Had she pushed too far? She was only trying to play along, not embarrass him. Glancing away from her cakes, she found him watching her, his lips in a tight smile as he shook his head, but his eyes were full of laughter. He understood what she was doing, and she flashed him a huge smile.

"Your sass is strong today." He pointed his piping bag at her. "But it's not going to help you beat me."

"We'll see about that."

Though they were given more time, Livvy felt the minutes went by quicker than in previous days. She barely got her final touches added before Adeline called the competition to a close and requested Will come to the front.

His cake and cupcakes looked amazing. Each layer of his cake was a version of one of the first four cakes he'd made in the competition, at least in design. Will had managed to make what should have looked disjointed at best flow effortlessly from one to the next.

Each layer featured a flavor from the final four cakes he'd created for the show. He'd done well in the previous days of competition, so the flavors needed only minor tweaking. Livvy was impressed. The finished product fit the theme well.

He stepped back, and Taylor called her to the front. She placed her cake on the table and stood before them with confidence.

"Today, I've created a cake that pays homage to not only the journey but those I walked beside on that journey. You'll note I incorporated ruffles since they are kind of my trademark. Instead of the typical polka dots, I added tiny orange-filled gelatin bubbles to reflect the personality of Harper and the flavors Evan and I used when we paired up for the farmer's market event.

"The cake is rich chocolate and cinnamon in honor of Nicholas, and the filling is an orange and ginger buttercream which, again, reflects the flavors Evan and I used. Enjoy."

Will and Livvy waited in silence for the judges to confer. After what seemed like hours, Adeline and Taylor stopped looking at each other and turned back to her and Will. She took a deep breath and closed her eyes. No matter what happened, she would be fine. She was proud of the cake she presented to them. It flawlessly included everything she loved about her time on the show. She opened her eyes as Adeline spoke.

"We've had to make tough decisions before, but today's was

the hardest yet. Will and Livvy, you are both excellent bakers. You took slightly different approaches to the theme for the day, with Will sticking closer to the themes of each competition and Livvy working in the relationships she developed along the way. Both offerings filled the requirements of today's assignments. And you both presented beautiful, precisely decorated cakes."

"You also expertly merged flavors from various days, creating cohesive flavor profiles for your cakes." Taylor interrupted. "There isn't a lot we can say in the negative about either cake. Again today, it comes down to which cake we think outshone the other by the slimmest of margins. It took a lot of discussion, but Adeline and I are prepared to announce our winner."

25

"Welcome to Arizona!" Isabel met Livvy as she exited the cab. "We're in the backyard. Papa is almost finished with the burgers, and the others are waiting."

She followed Isabel around the house.

"Welcome to my home." Nicholas lifted the spatula in a wave. "Drinks are in the cooler, and lunch is almost ready."

Livvy grabbed a bottle of water and made her way to the picnic table. Evan rose to meet her. As she stepped close, he wrapped his arms around her and kissed her cheek.

"You're not going to start that already, are you?" Will grumbled. "It's taken me the last eight months to erase the image of all your PDA during the competition. I don't need an instant replay."

"Good to see you, too." Livvy pulled away with a laugh. "How's the new shop going?"

Will shrugged. "A hundred grand helps get a new bakery started without as much to worry about, that's for sure. And the notoriety that comes with the win draws in customers, but we'll see how long that lasts."

"It'll last." Harper sipped her orange soda and sat beside him. "You're good at what you do."

"I know." He covered her hand with his own. "But thank you for your vote of confidence."

Livvy looked from their clasped hands to Harper, whose cheeks had gone pink. When had this happened, and why hadn't Harper told her about it? They talked at least two or three times a month. She raised an eyebrow, and Harper grinned.

"We've been talking since the show ended. He called to apologize for being a jerk, and I forgave him. Turns out there's more to Will than I first thought. We went on our first date when he came to visit a couple of weeks ago. I knew we would see you today, so I waited to surprise you."

"You definitely succeeded in doing that! I didn't expect it at all. And I'm happy for both of you."

"Thank you." Will smiled. "I thought a lot about your advice and realized you were right. I needed to just be me, and I felt like I owed everyone an apology. I only called to make things right and ended up with a great girlfriend to enjoy the journey with. But enough about us, how's it going with The Sugar Cube?"

"I thought it was going to be tough financially when I took all that time off work and didn't win. But you get noticed even if you come in second, especially with all the nice things the judges had to say about my work. I got back to more special orders than I've ever had in the winter months, and business has been growing steadily. I don't know how long it's going to last either, but I'm going to enjoy it while it does."

"But that's not the most exciting thing going on, is it?" Evan put his arm around her shoulders.

Nicholas interrupted with a plate of burgers. "Everyone grab a plate, and we'll say grace before Livvy gives us her exciting news."

Almost as soon as Nicholas said "amen," Harper turned to Livvy.

"Okay, now out with it. What's your news?"

With her burger halfway to her mouth, Livvy stopped. She

shrugged her shoulders and worked to keep a straight face. "Just that Evan is moving to St. Louis to help me with The Sugar Cube."

Nicholas looked between the two of them, his food momentarily forgotten on his plate. He finally settled his gaze on Evan. "Why didn't you tell me about this when you got here an hour ago? When are you moving? Have you found a place to stay?"

"I'll move up there in two months." Evan barely looked up. "I don't have to find a place. I'll be moving in with Livvy."

Isabel choked on her drink. Will and Harper set their burgers back on their plates. Silence reigned at the table. Evan squeezed Livvy's hand before picking up his burger for another bite. Livvy's gaze flitted from person to person around the table.

"Please don't be offended by this, but have you thought this through?" Nicholas cleared his throat. "I didn't think living together would mesh well with your beliefs. Has something changed?"

"It hasn't yet, but it will in two months." Evan smiled. "Livvy and I are getting married, and you're all invited to St. Louis for the wedding."

Harper's squeal sent neighborhood dogs into a frenzy. Livvy dutifully turned her ring diamond-side out and showed it off to a round of congratulations. Conversation revolved around wedding details for the remainder of lunch but moved on to other subjects once everyone had cleaned up and gathered at Nicholas's pool.

Evan and Will engaged in a race rematch, friendly this time. After Isabel left for work, Nicholas joined them, and Livvy was surprised to find he could hold his own against the younger swimmers. Harper cheered Will on from her deck chair.

Who would have guessed a reality baking competition would change her life? Only God could have known, and she would have to thank Tabitha again for the push to follow His leading.

He had even provided for her business to thrive in the wake of the show. She'd learned a lot about herself, made friends, and met—well, the man of her dreams.

Grand prize or not, Livvy's time on *Cake That* couldn't have been sweeter.

ABOUT THE AUTHOR

Heather Greer is a pastor's wife and preacher's kid from southern Illinois. While the characters she plucks from her imagination to put on the paper are purely fictional, you're likely to find little peaks into Heather's own interests on the page. From baking to crafting and Hallmark movies to sci-fi, readers will enjoy glimpses into Heather's life and loves. (And if you ever wonder, feel free to ask. Heather is just an email or Facebook message away. She'd love to hear from you!)

While these tidbits are fun, the most important element of life Heather brings to her stories is encouragement to live a life of faith. Heather's own faith has kept her through the good, the bad, and the ugly times in her life. God has grown her as a wife, mother, and friend through her experiences, and Heather knows God's purpose for her life is to challenge and cheer on others as they learn to let their faith in God shape who they are in everything life brings their way. Whether writing or speaking, Heather's prayer is that her desire to "encourage one another and build up one another" (1 Thessalonians 5:11, NASB) shines through.

MORE CONTEMPORARY FICTION FROM SCRIVENINGS PRESS

Bluebonnet Bride

Molly Noble Bull

Gina Hollister, a dyslexic with a PhD in educational psychology, is hired by widower and business tycoon, Steve Bryson, to tutor his fourteen-year-old daughter, Amanda, for the summer at his huge house near Durango, Colorado, a mansion that Gina calls a castle, and an attraction soon develops between Gina and Steve. However, their romance can never end in marriage because Gina believes the lies about Steve's womanizing told her by his ex-wife before she died. He claims he'll never marry again, even to a beautiful Bible Thumper like Dr. Gina Hollister.

A SOCIAL IMPACT NOVEL

Beneath the Seams

When success comes at a cost,
who pays the price?

Peyton H. Roberts

Beneath the Seams

Peyton H. Roberts

Fashion designer Shelby Lawrence is launching her mother-daughter dresses nationwide when she receives a photo of the girl who will change her life forever. Runa, the family's newly sponsored child, is a clever student growing up near Dhaka, Bangladesh. Shelby's daughter Paisley is instantly captivated by their faraway friend. As the girls exchange heartwarming messages, Shelby has no idea that a tragedy in Runa's life is about to upend her own.

Dresses are flying off the racks when a horrifying scene unfolds in Dhaka that threatens to destroy Shelby's pristine reputation. Even worse—it sends Runa's life spiraling down a terrifying path. Shelby must decide how far she's willing to go to right a tragic wrong.

Both a gripping exposé of fashion industry secrets and a heartwarming mother-daughter tale, Beneath the Seams explores love, conscience, hope, and the common threads connecting humanity.

Saving Grace

Amy R. Anguish

Michelle Wilson's one goal in life was to become a top journalist at the local paper in her hometown of Cedar Springs, Arkansas. But on the way to bringing that dream to reality, a life-changing wreck interrupts Michelle's plans and adds an orphaned baby into the mix. Now she has tough decisions ahead. Did God put her in that accident to save baby Grace? And if so, why is it so hard to convince everyone else she should be the baby's new mommy?

Greg Marshall has been Michelle's best friend his whole life. He's thrilled she's moving back home, but not so sure about her sudden desire to be a single mom. His feelings for her have grown through the years, but she's never seemed to notice. Can Greg help Michelle with the adoption and grow their relationship at the same time?

www.ingramcontent.com/pod-product-compliance
Lightning Source LLC
Chambersburg PA
CBHW070642100726
47907CB00007B/2077